Gabbie Flowers

And the Key to the Universe

*Addison
I send you
love
Dianne Caplin*

DIANNE CAPLIN

BALBOA
PRESS

A DIVISION OF HAY HOUSE

Balboa Press books may be ordered through booksellers or by contacting:

Balboa Press
A Division of Hay House
1663 Liberty Drive
Bloomington, IN 47403
www.balboapress.com
1 (877) 407-4847

Because of the dynamic nature of the Internet, any web addresses or links contained in this book may have changed since publication and may no longer be valid. The views expressed in this work are solely those of the author and do not necessarily reflect the views of the publisher, and the publisher hereby disclaims any responsibility for them.

The author of this book does not dispense medical advice or prescribe the use of any technique as a form of treatment for physical, emotional, or medical problems without the advice of a physician, either directly or indirectly. The intent of the author is only to offer information of a general nature to help you in your quest for emotional and spiritual well-being. In the event you use any of the information in this book for yourself, which is your constitutional right, the author and the publisher assume no responsibility for your actions.

Any people depicted in stock imagery provided by Thinkstock are models, and such images are being used for illustrative purposes only.
Certain stock imagery © Thinkstock.

Printed in the United States of America.

ISBN: 978-1-4525-2142-8 (sc)
ISBN: 978-1-4525-2140-4 (hc)
ISBN: 978-1-4525-2141-1 (e)

Library of Congress Control Number: 2014915752

Balboa Press rev. date: 10/29/2014

For Rick, my love, who always believed in Gabbie.

Contents

Chapter One

The Girl Who Flies

G abbie did not *no considerar* consider herself a freak, even though, on more than one occasion she had been described as such.

She did not have superhuman powers, even though her soul flew through the night sky while her body lay sleeping in bed. Anyone's soul could fly. All they had to do was believe. And Gabbie believed.

Though she could fly anywhere in the universe, there was only one place Gabbie wanted to go. Heaven.

When she was four, her mother, Katherine, died, severing her silver cord permanently. But that didn't stop them from spending time together. Every night, after Gabbie fell asleep her soul would slip from her body and race towards the pink sky where she knew her mother would be waiting.

That's where we were when Gabbie's silver cord, which was attached to her belly began to glow. It was a warning

1

that any second her soul would return to the brownstone in New York City, where she lived with her grandmother, Alice Curtis and her sister, Victoria.

"*Oh drats,*" Gabbie said. "I don't wanna go just yet."

But there was nothing I could do. It was my job to make sure her soul was where it needed to be, and right now it needed to be back in her body before the alarm clock in her bedroom rang.

And who am I, you ask?

I'm Gabbie's guide, keeper of her sacred scroll. She calls me Samuel.

My official title is: Spirit Guide. I know, it sounds impressive, but I'm not some enlightened being. I'm just an average soul, like Gabbie, except I live in another dimension. It's called *Here*. And *Here* looks just like *there*, but only a million times better. And where is *Here?* It's actually just three feet above *there*, though it vibrates so quickly I'm virtually invisible to all but a few. And Gabbie, she's one of the few.

Before Gabbie was born, I took an oath. I promised to guide her through her life to the best of my ability. I know every choice she could make, every road she could go down. But I can never, ever, interfere or hinder her plan in anyway. All I can do is make suggestions, try to make her life as smooth as possible. But ultimately, her life is her decision.

"I'll see you tomorrow," Gabbie said to her mother. A moment later, her soul was yanked from *here* towards *there*.

"I love you!" Katherine shouted, but the wall between her and her daughter, was now too thick for her daughter to hear. She looked at me, her slender fingers rubbing the golden key hanging around her neck. The token has given her comfort in times of trouble and the simple gesture told me more than words could say. She was worried.

According to Gabbie's scroll, a fork in her path is coming, and if truth be told, if fear were to consume her, things could get bad. Very very very bad.

"Don't worry Katherine, I got this." With a wink, I assured her, "She'll be fine."

As we flew through the space between dimensions Gabbie asked, "Can we take the scenic route?" She crossed her fingers and batted her big brown eyes. "Please."

"All right. But we need to make it fast, okay?" I said.

Gabbie shot ahead of me like one of the rockets her father builds. His name is Michael. He lives in Florida. After the car accident that took Katherine's life he was so overwhelmed by grief, and his job at the space center, it was impossible to properly care for his two young daughters, so Nana volunteered to raise them. They spent every holiday and vacation together, and one day Gabbie hoped they could all live together again.

As we soared through the sky, the sun was beginning to peek over the skyscrapers that loomed over the city. We shot down towards Central Park, where the trees burst with new life. Tiny clusters of bright lime leaves covered the limbs of the elm and maple trees. Pink and white flowers graced the branches of the dogwood trees. Wild crocuses pushed through the hard ground searching for the warmth of the sun, their purple petals stretching toward the sky.

The streets were quiet except for the squeal of a distant garbage truck. As we took a sharp left turn around a fifty-story building, we headed south toward Greenwich Village. Gabbie was ahead of me. I liked to let her think she could fly faster than I could.

She looked back at me. "Hurry up, slow poke!" she laughed.

I squinted my green eyes and gritted my teeth to make it look like I was flying as fast as I could. She threw her head back and laughed again.

When we approached her brownstone on W. 11th Street, Gabbie rolled into a tight little ball.

Swish!

She dropped like a cannonball through the roof. I dove in after her, headfirst. We passed through the attic filled with old junk that Nana Alice didn't have the heart to get rid of. There was the highchair the girls used before they came to live there, along with Gabbie's tricycle, Victoria's scooter, and a steamer trunk plastered with stickers from faraway places. Gabbie had once said she wanted to visit each place and according to her sacred chart, I was certain she could do it.

Inside the trunk were fancy dress-up clothes. Gabbie loved to play dress-up, but Victoria, two years her senior, didn't have the time or the desire to play the games they used to play. "I'm thirteen," she said, "too old to pretend I'm a princess." Or a movie star. Or an heiress, like one of those rich ladies who lived in a fancy penthouse apartment on Fifth Avenue. She'd rather read or text her friends.

Gabbie tried to talk me into playing dress-up, but I refused. I told her it wasn't in my job description. A guy had to preserve his dignity, after all. So the old fur stoles and yards of costume pearls gathered dust instead of applause and laughter.

As Gabbie's soul passed through her bedroom ceiling, she flailed her arms trying to steer to the left. I knew that at this rate she'd miss her body completely and pass right through Victoria, who was standing over her bed blowing hard into a whistle. I gave Gabbie a shove. Thankfully, it worked. Her soul missed her sister and crashed into her own body sleeping in bed. I don't know which would be worse—passing through a human body or listening to Gabbie's complaints about passing through a human body. It's nothing to pass through something that isn't alive, but it's awful to pass through something with a heartbeat and a brain.

Gabbie's eyes popped open the minute her soul fussed with her shell. She was back. And just in the nick of time.

Chapter Two

The Invisible Boy

ictoria gave the whistle a final blast. Gabbie clamped her hands over her ears. It was the third time this week she had slept through her alarm.

When the whistle ceased Victoria said, "You'd better hurry up. Breakfast is ready." She put the whistle on top of her dresser and headed down the staircase. Her footsteps were light as she floated down the stairs. Gabbie, on the other hand, could wake the dead. She stomped down the stairs like a herd of elephants, causing everything in the house to shake.

Excited to share her adventure, Gabbie threw the covers off the bed and raced across the room, her footsteps heavy even in bare feet. Nana had tried, unsuccessfully, to teach her youngest granddaughter to tread lightly, to glide instead of stomp, but she had had no luck. If there were one consolation, it was that Nana always knew where Gabbie was and what she was up to.

Gabbie picked the uniform she had worn the day before off the floor. With a whiff she checked to see if it was clean enough to wear.

"What?" she asked me, as I stuck my finger in my mouth and pretended to gag. "I'm eleven. I don't stink yet."

She tugged a white button-down blouse over her head. She didn't bother undoing the buttons; it took too much time. She ran her hands over the school's patch sewn on the chest pocket hoping to smooth out the wrinkles. The school's emblem hadn't changed since her mother went to Saint Bernadette's when she was Gabbie's age. A green and blue plaid skirt lay on the floor. "I hate this skirt," Gabbie mumbled as she kicked it up to her hand.

I know, but you have to wear it, I said. My voice echoed inside her head. Now that I was in her dimension, I could only talk to her telepathically. She turned her skirt inside out and pulled it on. The white lining of the pockets stuck out like rabbit ears.

You can't wear it that way, I laughed.

She raised her eyebrows as if to challenge me. "All they said is that I had to wear it. They didn't say how."

My lips rose in a smile making the dimples in my cheeks deep. I must admit she had a point.

Gabbie plopped down on the bed. In her hand was a pair of white socks. She rolled on one, then the other. The right sock drooped sadly into the heel of her patent-leather shoe. She tried rolling it up, but it didn't stay. She shrugged her shoulders. "Whatever," she said.

She had the same attitude about her hair. Fine as corn silk and just as blonde, it stuck straight off her forehead. She dragged a wet comb through her bangs, but they still didn't behave.

Nana called up the stairwell. "Let's go, Gabbie! Breakfast is ready!"

Gabbie grabbed her backpack and took off down the stairs. It still amazed me how one little girl could make so much noise. With each heavy step, the plates in the cupboard rattled and the silverware in the drawers clanked. The pictures on the walls jiggled, and the doors wobbled on their hinges.

This was my first crack at this guide thing. And let me tell you, being in charge of someone's life was stressful. Gabbie could be so stubborn at times that even though she knew I would never steer her wrong, she still ignored me.

Take this moment for instance. Even though her Nana told her a million times, Gabbie did what she always did. I warned her not to do it, but she did it anyway.

BAM!

For a second everything was eerily still. Then—just like yesterday and the day before that, and the day before that—Nana hollered, "Gabriella Flowers, what have I told you about jumping down the stairs?"

Then—just like yesterday and the day before that, and the day before that—Gabbie said, "I'm okay. Everything's fine."

Nana stood next to the stove holding her heart. She took a few deep breaths as Gabbie entered the kitchen. Even though Gabbie knew heaven was just a flight away, the thought of something happening to her Nana brought an unexplained pain to her heart. "I'm sorry. I didn't mean to scare you," Gabbie said. She reached up on her tiptoes and kissed her Nana's cheek. It was soft and smelled of fresh soap.

Though it was only seven thirty in the morning, Nana had already done her yoga. She traded her jeans for yoga pants and started practicing as a way to handle her new life's stress. It had been many years since she raised her only daughter, Katherine, and Gabbie, well, she was a totally different soul.

Nana kept her hair short. It was white and stood straight off her head with the help of a firm sticky gel. Though her starched cotton blouses had been abandoned for soft T-shirts, she continued to wear the pearl earrings Papa Jim had given her right before he died.

Though Gabbie hadn't known Papa Jim when he had been *there* in her dimension, she had danced with him *here,* in heaven. "He was so light on his feet," Gabbie had said to Nana the morning after they met. "It was like dancing on a cloud."

Nana started to turn back to tend to the oatmeal bubbling on the stove when she jerked her head back to have another look at Gabbie. "Is your skirt on inside out?"

"Yes it is," Gabbie said proudly. She took the bowl of oatmeal from her grandmother and joined her sister at the table.

"You can't wear your skirt inside out," Victoria said, obviously disgusted. She was the polar opposite of Gabbie. She was impeccably dressed. Her collar was firm and her auburn hair was perfectly combed. "It's against the rules."

Gabbie shoveled a spoonful of oatmeal into her mouth. "Nowhere in the school's handbook does it say I can't wear it like this. I checked," she said.

Victoria looked down her nose, which was small and turned up on the end. "That might be true, but the other kids are gonna think you're a freak."

"I don't care what other people think," Gabbie said, though I knew that wasn't true. She *did* care—especially when it came to Melissa Graves, the meanest girl in school.

You might want to change. This could result in some unnecessary pain, I said. Gabbie excused herself and ran from the table, claiming she had to use the bathroom. A few moments later she was back, skirt turned right side out.

Victoria smiled. It was a victorious grin.

I took a seat next to Gabbie at the table. I don't eat. I don't have to. But that doesn't mean I can't. I could, if I wanted to. After all, the food in heaven is to die for. I cringed. Sorry, no pun intended.

Gabbie shoveled another heaping spoonful of oatmeal into her mouth. "You'll never believe where I went last night," she said with her mouth full. Victoria rolled her eyes as she always did when Gabbie talked of our adventures.

"Samuel took me to the *Hall of Reconnection*. It was totally awesome. I saw Mama there. She looked so beautiful—like she did when she was alive, only prettier. It was like she... *glowed*."

"Oh, please, it was just a dream," Victoria said in her usual tone. It was like ... yeah, right. Who believes you fly through the sky like a bird when everyone else is sleeping?

"It wasn't a dream! It was real!" Gabbie said. Her face turned bright red and the veins popped out of her neck. She balled her fists up and I knew she was fighting the urge to slam them down on the table. She looked at Nana for help. "Tell her, Nana. Tell her it's real."

Victoria did that eye-rolling thing. "Really, Gabbie. Don't you think it's about time you stop believing in your imaginary friend? You're eleven years old."

After Katherine died, Nana had read every book about *here* she could get her hands on. That's where she learned about spirit guides and astral traveling. So when Gabbie started talking about the blonde-haired boy that no one else could see, Nana encouraged her to talk to me. And let me tell you, I couldn't be more thankful. I can't imagine how difficult it must be for those guides whose humans don't know they exist. Take Victoria's guide, Madeline, for instance. She faded from Victoria's memory when Victoria was about four years old. Katherine closed the door, sealing Madeline out. That's how it usually happens. A kid talks about his or her spirit guide, and because grown-ups can no longer see through the veil of dimensions, they just assume the kid has an imaginary friend. But let me tell you—we *are* real. R-e-a-l. *Real!*

Madeline, who was hovering directly above Victoria, sighed. Even Nana tried to help. "Do you believe in air?" Nana said.

"Yes," Victoria huffed. She knew where her grandmother was headed, but it didn't do any good. Nothing she or Gabbie could say would convince Victoria that I really do exist and that Gabbie's soul did leave her body at night to fly. But it didn't make it any less true.

With a bowl full of oatmeal and a hot cup tea, Nana Alice started to sit down in the chair I was occupying. Gabbie yelled, "Don't sit there! Samuel is sitting there." Though invisible to everyone else, to Gabbie, I appear solid, just like a human.

I wanted to move, to get up before Nana sat on me, but that would mean I would have to go straight through her. Either way, it was going to be awful. My hands braced the side of the chair, anticipating the swishing of her blood flowing through her veins and the pounding of her heart in my ears. Her thoughts would explode in my head like cannons. Luckily, Nana caught herself before I merged with her body. "Oh, I beg your pardon," she laughed as the teacup rattled on its saucer. She took the chair next to me. Her guide, Two Feathers (though the headdress he wore had dozens of them) laughed, too. I sighed with relief. Victoria sighed, too, but not for the same reason. She gathered her breakfast dishes and headed for the sink.

Gabbie didn't know it, but it wasn't really *me* Victoria had a problem with. Madeline once told me that every time Gabbie mentioned their mother's name, a wave of emotion rushed through her sister like a giant tsunami. She missed her mother so, but unlike Gabbie she didn't believe she could fly. So her soul stayed cooped up in her body just waiting for the day she could be freed.

Nana, however, saw the pain in Victoria's eyes. She placed her finger against her lips, telling Gabbie to wait until her sister was out of the room to continue her story.

Gabbie tapped her spoon against the table impatiently as Victoria rinsed her dish, then placed it in the dishwasher. She wiped off her hands, pulling the dishcloth down each finger. She had the tendency to chaff and wanted to make sure they were dry.

"Good God, would you hurry up?" Gabbie mumbled.

When Victoria finally left the room, Gabbie sighed with relief. I don't know how much longer she could have waited without losing her mind.

She told Nana how I took her to a huge building. "It had giant gold columns that led to a pair of large brass doors. " She paused. "Did you know there were buildings in heaven?" It wasn't really a question because she didn't wait for Nana to answer. She just plowed on with her story. "It looked like one of those ancient buildings in Greece. You know, the ..." Again she paused. She tapped her finger on her chin. The name of the building with massive marble columns escaped her.

Before I could remind her, Nana beat me to it. "You mean the Parthenon?" she asked.

Gabbie snapped her fingers. "That's it! The Parthenon. Samuel told me that all the ancient structures on Earth are really only replicas of the great halls in heaven. He said the angels gave the human architects the inspiration to build them here. And the gardens ... Oh, Nana, they were *soooo* beautiful. As far as the eye could see, there were flowers, and it smelled *soooo* good."

The cuckoo popped out of the clock hanging on the kitchen wall. If there was time, Nana would read the tealeaves stuck to the bottom of Gabbie's teacup before she left for school. Gabbie loved hearing her fortune. She gulped down the remaining tea then handed the cup to Nana. Victoria didn't believe in fortune telling, so her teacup was placed in the dishwasher, leaves unread.

Nana took the cup and twirled it three times. The tealeaves scattered around the inside. Then she placed the teacup on the saucer, bottom facing up. After a few seconds, Nana slowly turned the cup right side up. Gabbie leaned over her shoulder and peered curiously into the cup. "Well, what do you see?" she asked excitedly.

Dianne Caplin

I leaned in, too.

Nana's brows scrunched together in concentration.

"Well?" Gabbie asked. She tapped her fingers against the table in anticipation.

"I see a cake, here, near the rim." Nana pointed to the clump of leaves hanging on the edge of the cup. "And a box, here."

Gabbie peered inside the teacup. "Are you sure?" she asked. "It just looks like a bunch of brown blobs."

I totally agreed with Gabbie. I had no idea how Nana could use those tiny brown speckles to tell the future. But she did—and with amazing accuracy.

"I'm sure of it. A cake and a present," Nana said with certainty.

"My birthday is months away, so why would there be a cake and presents?" Gabbie asked.

It's the way the universe speaks, in symbols, you know, like in images, or pictures, I told her.

"Oh," she said. "But that still doesn't explain it."

Nana clapped her hands together. "It's a gift. The spirit world is sending you a gift," she said delightedly.

Nana had no idea how right she was.

14

Chapter Three
The Tall and Short of It

The city had come alive. The traffic in the streets was thick and buzzing. Business people hurried to work, deliverymen unloaded their wares, and taxi drivers honked their horns.

Gabbie burst out the front door, startling Mr. Fiddlydinks, the neighborhood stray. He was rolled up in a ball fast asleep in the corner of the porch. It had become his favorite spot. I don't know why. Every morning, Gabbie made the cat jump out of its skin, and today was no different. His black fur stood on end, and his claws stuck out of his white-socked feet. A long whining meow warned her to stay away. Gabbie stuck her tongue out at him and then jumped up on the wall separating the stoops. Gone were the days of trying to befriend him.

When Mr. Fiddlydinks first appeared on the stoop looking for a hand out, Gabbie begged Nana to take him in, but Victoria was allergic to his dander. So Gabbie had to settle for what she could get, which turned out to more trouble than it was worth. After a few infected bites on her fingers and too many scratches to count, she gave up trying to earn his trust.

As Gabbie waited for her friends—Melissa Graves and Camille Wilson—two dragonflies settled on the edge of the wall.

One blue.

One green.

"That's weird," Gabbie said. "I remember when we lived with Daddy. Dragonflies were everywhere. But I never saw one, let alone two, here in the middle of New York City!"

She wasn't the only one who was intrigued by the pair. Mr. Fiddlydinks' tail swayed as he stared at the dragonflies. He was ready to pounce. Gabbie waved her hand at him trying to get his attention. "*Psst*, go away," she whispered to the old cat. But he didn't listen. Instead, he jumped into the air, paws stretched out toward the dragonflies, hoping to make them his morning meal.

"Oh no!" Gabbie shouted. Anticipating a crash, she squeezed her eyes shut. The last time Mr. Fiddlydinks jumped over the retaining wall, it had cost her twenty dollars.

It had been a lovely day, and Gabbie's nervous energy had been making Nana Alice batty. She had sent Gabbie outside to get some fresh air before she lost her mind. It wasn't long before Gabbie got bored. She already bounced her ball against the edge of the steps and counted all the cars parked at the curb. There were four blue ones, two red, three silver, and nine black. After she counted the cars, she jumped from the stoop trying to go further each time until she twisted her ankle. But the pain didn't last and soon she was twirling. Faster and faster she spun until she lost her balance. She bumped into the wall separating the stoop and startled Mr. Fiddlydinks. He jumped to the ground, taking Mr. Warsinski's prized orchid with him.

Gabbie stood behind Nana, gripping her dress as Mr. Warsinski ranted and raved. His round belly shook. His bald head was bright red, and the veins in his neck looked as though they might explode at any moment.

He thought Gabbie needed more discipline. "You need to send her to Saint Anne's. There she'd get a proper upbringing."

Saint Anne's was a school for girls. Bad girls. Girls worse than Melissa Graves.

There had to be a way to make it up to Mr. Warsinski. She didn't like the idea of him being mad at her, or going to Saint Anne's. So she took twenty dollars out of her piggy bank and went down to the flower stand on the corner to buy a new plant for her next-door neighbor. He grumbled a bit when she gave it to him, but she could tell he liked it. That had made her feel good.

Thankfully, this time Mr. Fiddlydinks didn't break anything. Gabbie only had ten dollars left and she was saving up to buy Nana something special for her birthday, although she knew a card would do. Nana still carried around the card Gabbie made for her birthday the year before, and every chance her Nana had to show it off she pulled it from her purse.

Mr. Fiddlydinks did, however, send the dragonflies into flight.

"Oh, drats!" Gabbie said. "Why can't that stupid old cat find somewhere else to sleep?"

The morning sun peeked through the city buildings, making it hard for Gabbie to locate the dragonflies. She shaded her eyes hoping to get a better view. "Where did they go?" she said, peering up into the sky.

Melissa Graves stood at the bottom of the stairs laughing. She had a large bellowing laugh, just right for someone so long and lanky.

Oh brother, here's trouble, I mumbled.

"What are you doing?" she asked. "Talking to your imaginary friend?"

Her skinny brown hair clung to her skinny pale face. Her breakfast was still clinging to the braces on her teeth. Gabbie rolled her lips in and rubbed her belly. The egg hanging off Melissa's braces was only partly to blame for nausea stirring in Gabbie's stomach. I knew she wished she had never told Melissa about me. At the time she thought it would help if Melissa and Camille knew they too had spirit guides, but all it did was make Melissa laugh—just like her spirit guide Dean thought she would. However, Camille had been intrigued. And since Gabbie could only see me, I told her to tell Camille what her spirit guide looked like.

"Your guide has curly brown hair and lots of freckles. And her name is Mildred," Gabbie repeated to Camille.

Camille gasped. "Just like me!"

Melissa shook her head in disbelief. "Are you kidding? Now *you* have an imaginary friend, too? What are you people—*five*?" she laughed. And laughed. And laughed.

I didn't bother to tell Gabbie what Dean looked like. It wouldn't have mattered to Melissa that his skin was dark, and his eyes were even darker. He could be a Cyclops with florescent green skin for all she knew. It didn't matter back then, and it wouldn't matter now.

Dean had tried to persuade Melissa to keep that conversation between the three of them, but the minute Melissa entered the schoolyard she told everyone that Gabbie had an invisible friend.

I tried to get Gabbie to laugh it off because the truth was she *did* have an invisible friend, but Gabbie didn't "see" it that way, resulting in a stomachache that had lasted a whole week.

That was the first time her mother had sent her a penny from heaven. Since Gabbie couldn't see or hear her mother on this side of the veil, it was a good way for Katherine to show Gabbie she was there.

We had been in the schoolyard. The penny bounced on the pavement, right in front of Gabbie's feet. *It's from your mom. Look at the date,* I said. The date stamped on the penny was the same year her mother had been born.

A smile broke across Gabbie's face. "How does she do that?"

I shrugged. "I don't know." And I still don't. With all my practice, I've yet to master the skill of moving objects through dimensions. I've tried and tried and tried, but I still can't seem to get the knack of it.

Now, as the girls stood on the sidewalk outside Gabbie's house, Camille tried to explain spirit guides to Melissa. "They're not imaginary. They just happen to live in another dimension." She looked at Gabbie for approval. Gabbie nodded.

Melissa laughed. "I guess now that you're wearing those stupid glasses, you can see invisible things too."

Camille failed the annual eye examine, resulting in a pair of bright red spectacles. She pushed them up the bridge of her nose. "No, I can't."

Melissa shook her head in disgust. "You're as freaky as she is." She hitched her thumb at Gabbie.

"Hey now, there's no reason for name-calling," I said, pointing at Melissa.

Dean cupped his hands and placed them next to Melissa's ear. "Melissa, it's in your soul's best interest to be kind!" he shouted. But it was obvious that Melissa either didn't hear a word Dean said, or she totally ignored him, because she pulled back her hand, and before Dean could tell her *no*, she gave Camille a shove.

"*Hey*," Mildred said. She grabbed Camille by the shoulders and steadied her. Camille wobbled but didn't fall down.

Dean dropped his head. "Sorry about that. It's like talking to a stump."

If I didn't know the reason behind this friendship, I would be telling Gabbie to run as fast as she could. But there was a reason for it, and all I could hope for was that it would be over as quickly and as painlessly as possible.

The moment Gabbie noticed the cylinder tucked in Melissa's backpack she got a sinking feeling in the pit of her stomach. "Is that your entry for the mural contest?" she asked, even though she knew it was.

A grin slowly broke across Melissa's face. "I wouldn't waste any more time on your entry; I got the winner right here," she said, patting the tube proudly.

Gabbie gagged and grabbed her stomach. I didn't know if it was because there was still egg stuck between her friend's teeth or because she still hadn't come up with an idea grand enough to win the contest. A pile of crumbled up mural attempts sat in the waste paper basket in the corner of her room, none of which she thought were worthy of the grand prize. If she was going to win, she better think of something soon. She only had a few days left before the deadline.

With her chin held high, Melissa marched down the street. Her limbs poked out in weird angles. "Let's go, freaks. We're going to be late."

Gabbie and Camille hurried behind her. Camille, with her short chubby legs, practically had to jog to keep up. She pushed her glasses up off the end of her nose while struggling to keep her backpack in place. The blush in her cheeks made it hard to see the freckles sprinkled across her face.

As they hurried down the avenue, Camille grabbed Gabbie's arm, stopping her dead in her tracks.

"What is it?" Gabbie asked. "Are you having an asthma attack?" It wouldn't have been the first time Camille had struggled to breathe.

"I'm fine," Camille grunted as she worked at dislodging something shiny that was stuck in the sidewalk. She hooted as she produced the object. "Look, a penny!" she said proudly.

Melissa came to a halt, her face scrunched up with disgust. "Are you kidding me? We're going to be late because of a stupid *penny*?"

"Maybe an angel left it for me," Camille said. She brought the penny to her lips, kissed it, and shoved it into her skirt pocket.

Melissa raised her fist. "Angel *schmangel*. If we're late because of that penny, you're gonna need more than an angel to help you," she growled.

The girls hurried down the busy city street weaving their way in and out of the morning crowd. Although the sidewalk was teeming with pedestrians, a man dressed completely in green caught Gabbie's attention. She scrunched her brows together and her mouth hung open as she looked at him. His suit was glistening in the morning sunlight. It sparkled as if it were made completely of tiny jewels. He tipped his hat to Gabbie as he approached. "Good day," he said.

Gabbie couldn't help staring at the man in the shimmering green suit. He wasn't a very big man, maybe five feet eight at the very most. His features were flat and spread wide across his face. And his eyes looked too big for his head.

Behind the man walked a young woman. Her blue dress sparkled and flowed gracefully as she seemed to float effortlessly down the sidewalk.

"Lovely day," the woman said as she passed by Gabbie. Her hair was so blonde it looked almost white, and her eyes were large like the man's eyes, but instead of green like his, hers were blue. Pale blue. Like the icebergs Gabbie had just studied in science class.

Gabbie turned to have one last look, but to her surprise both the man and the woman were gone. She gasped.

"What's wrong now?" Melissa said. Thankfully, she didn't slow her pace. She just kept on walking.

"Did you see them? Where did they go?" Gabbie whispered to Camille.

"See *who*?" Camille whispered back.

Standing on her tiptoes, Gabbie tried to look over the morning rush. "The woman in the blue sparkly dress and the man dressed in the green shimmery suit." Her voice was still hushed.

Camille raised her chin, trying to look over the crowd. Men in dark suits and ladies in black dresses hurried down the sidewalk. There were moms pushing baby strollers and a dog walker struggling to keep a half a dozen canines in line. There were deliverymen and other students, some dressed in uniforms and some not. But there wasn't a woman in a sparkly blue dress or a man in a shimmery green suit. They seemed to have vanished into thin air.

Since Gabbie didn't ask me who they were or where they had gone, I couldn't volunteer any information. I just hoped we would never see them again, because if they showed up, it would mean things would have taken a turn for the worse.

Chapter Four
The Seed

Every wall in the entire school was painted the same color, puke green. But soon, the puke green wall next to the auditorium doors would be decorated by this year's winning mural.

Gabbie stood and stared at the wall. Her eyes narrowed. A good twenty seconds went by and she still hadn't blinked.

What are you doing? I asked. I couldn't imagine why she was staring at the ugly green wall.

"I'm doing that thing you told me to do," she said not taking her eyes from the wall.

And what might that be? I asked, confused.

"I'm trying to visualize my mural here. It would be a heck of a lot easier if I knew what it looked like."

You'd better get to class. The bell is about to ring, I told her. She was so busy daydreaming about her mural entry she was almost late for class.

Just as the bell began to ring, Gabbie raced into the classroom and slid sideways into her chair. It tipped to the side but she caught her balance before tumbling to the floor.

"Very graceful," Melissa scoffed. Her lanky limbs poked out from beneath the desk like a daddy longlegs balancing on the head of a pin.

"I give it a seven," Camille laughed, holding up one finger too many.

"That's *eight*, you dweeb," Melissa said, shaking her head.

Camille double-checked her fingers, counting them again. "Ten, nine, eight, seven?" She rolled her thumb in and looked at the six fingers remaining. She shook her head and started over, this time starting at one. She peeled open each finger until she arrived at seven, displaying them proudly.

"Again, *five*?" Melissa barked.

Camille stuck her tongue out when Melissa wasn't looking.

Gabbie stifled a giggle. I did, too. It wouldn't have been wise to have her hear me laugh.

Mrs. Jones, their fifth grade teacher, stood in the front of the classroom smacking erasers together. She coughed as chalk dust filled the air. It settled on her hair, making her brown bun look grey. She coughed again as it clung to her glasses, and her dress. It coated her desk like a dusting of snow.

Melissa laughed. "She's such a dweeb."

Dean produced a giant megaphone and held it to Melissa's ear. "It's not kind to call people names!" he shouted. She batted her hand next to her ear. I raised my brows, impressed. Maybe he was onto something.

Mrs. Jones waved her arms, trying to clear the air. "Today ... *cough, cough.* In honor of the annual mural contest, we're going to discuss art through the ages." *Cough, cough, cough.*

There it was again, the look of panic on Gabbie's face. I knew she was worried. If she didn't think of something soon, her dream of winning the mural contest would simply fade away like the dust that finally settled to the floor. I wanted to tell her, "Relax, everything is cool." But I couldn't. Besides, I didn't want to spoil the surprise.

Gabbie's elbows came to rest on her desk with a thump. She cradled her head in her hands and tried to pay attention, but every time the teacher said the word *artist* or *painting*, Gabbie's brows knitted together and she let out a grunt.

Don't worry, I'm sure you'll think of something, I said trying to reassure her. I knew for a fact she would. It was in the plan. It said so in her sacred contract.

I sat next to Mildred and Dean on the heater, which stretched beneath the giant windows. Mildred picked at her fingernails. Even though Camille couldn't see her, at least she entertained the idea. Whereas, I felt bad for Dean; he definitely had his hands full guiding Melissa. He leaned his chin on his fist and sighed. The other students' guides were scattered throughout the classroom. Some sat on their responsibilities' desks while others hovered above them. Collette, Mrs. Jones' guide, was so pale she looked as if she too, was covered in dust. Her milky skin almost looked blue. One minute in the sunlight and she would ignite like a vampire. I don't know why she still wears that gigantic hoop dress with all its pearls and lace. And that hairdo! It's piled so high on her head she hardly fits through a doorway. But it's the beauty mark drawn on her cheek that I don't understand. What makes her think a coal black dot drilled into the side of her face can make her look anything but ridiculous?

Mrs. Jones pulled down the white screen above the blackboard, and coughed. The class broke out in excited whispers. They loved when Mrs. Jones put on a slide show. Instead of using the Internet and a flat screen TV like the other teachers used, Mrs. Jones fired up an ancient slide projector.

"I bet Mrs. Jones is older than that projector," Melissa said, as the teacher wheeled the projector from the closet. The teacher asked Noel, a dark-haired boy who was good at athletics, to lower the blinds.

The blinds were as old, if not older, than the projector. Noel unwound the cord holding the blinds in place and deliberately let it slip from his grip. He squeezed his blue eyes shut and drew up his shoulders, anticipating a bang. The blinds crashed against the windowsill and the students jumped. Noel laughed. "Sorry," he said, although he really wasn't.

As soon as Mrs. Jones turned on the projector, the air filled with a faint burning odor. She coughed.

"Something's burning," Melissa snickered. "I hope the thing blows up."

Gabbie's eyes grew wide. She looked at me.

It's just old—nothing to worry about, I told her.

Noel turned out the lights, but not before making them flick a few times. Mrs. Jones thanked him and sent him back to his seat, which was directly in front of Gabbie. The shadow of his fingers made a rabbit as he passed through the light streaming from the projector. Behind the rabbit, his other hand formed an alligator. With a chomp, the alligator ate the rabbit. The whole class laughed.

"Okay, settle down," the teacher said. She took some slides out of a rusty tin box and slid them into the old projector.

Dust motes floated through the stream of light. Noel turned around in his seat and whispered to Gabbie. "You know what dust is made of, don't you?" He began to laugh. "Dried up skin."

Gabbie crinkled her nose. "That's disgusting," she said.

Noel laughed. "It's true," he said, turning to face the front of the room.

The projector hummed. A black and white drawing of a man with a long bushy beard appeared on the screen. "Can anyone tell me who this is?" asked the teacher.

I smiled. Just the other day, (your time not mine), I saw Michelangelo working on another masterpiece when I visited the *Temple of Artistic Endeavors*. In the dimension called *here*, time didn't exist; it was always the present. In the picture on the screen, Michelangelo appeared to be much older than he does *here*.

The room remained quiet. I jumped from the heater and rushed to whisper in Gabbie's ear. She raised her hand cautiously. When Mrs. Jones nodded toward her, Gabbie repeated what I had told her.

"Is it *Michelangelo?*" she asked, as if doubting me.

The teacher's eyebrows rose with surprise. "Why yes, it *is* Michelangelo. Very good, Miss Flowers."

Gabbie looked at me as I resumed my seat on the heater, her eyes as huge as saucers. I stretched my legs out and cupped my hands behind my head. *I can't believe you still doubt me,* I said.

By the end of the morning lesson, Mrs. Jones had covered another Renaissance master, Leonardo da Vinci—also from Italy and who lived during the same time as Michelangelo. She also discussed two master impressionists, Claude Monet, and Vincent van Gogh.

Leo   Mic   Claude   Vincent

Chapter Five
Lunch

*P*aper airplanes circled the cafeteria as the lunch attendants tried desperately to resume order. A crowd of boys teased an elderly aide by pitching pennies on the floor only to watch her bend over to pick them up. Muttering something about *ungrateful hoodlums*, the round old woman shoved the coins deep into her pocket. Another group of students took advantage of the distracted aide and tossed pickles towards the ceiling hoping to get them to stick.

Gabbie was mid-bite into her first bite of sandwich when Melissa announced she was done. She shoved the remaining bit of sandwich in her mouth. Then she grabbed Camille's sandwich from her hand, threw it on her tray, and marched toward the trash receptacle. She was headed out to the playground, no doubt to secure the jump rope. Dean followed her, trying to persuade her to be nice.

Camille sighed, "I wasn't done yet." Mildred placed her hands on Camille's shoulder trying to soothe her.

Gabbie ripped her sandwich in half and handed it to her. "Here, you can share mine."

Mildred looked at me. "She's so sweet," she said.

I agreed.

The girls shoved the sandwiches into their mouths and hurried to catch up with Melissa. If they did what she said, maybe—just maybe—this would be the day they got the chance to jump.

Melissa stood in the middle of the basketball court with one hand on her hip while she twirled the rope in the other. The boys who were playing basketball had to dribble around her. She stood several inches above the tallest boy, and the sneer on her face and the rope in her hand kept them from crossing her. "Do you have a problem?" she snarled.

Most of the lunch period passed and neither Gabbie nor Camille had gotten a chance to jump. Both girls were getting tired. They were getting tired of not having a turn, and tired of Melissa's complaints.

"You need to turn the rope faster. You need to turn the rope higher. You turn the rope like a girl," Melissa whined.

"I *am* a girl," Camille sniffled, pushing her glasses up off the end of her nose.

Camille was not one bit athletic. Her arms were weak as wet tissue, and she was hardly able to swing the rope in a complete circle. Gabbie tried really hard to correct the rope. Sometimes it snapped. Sometimes it jerked. But, thank goodness, she always managed to get it high enough to clear Melissa's head.

"When can *we* jump?" Camille whined. She held her aching shoulder as she turned the rope. Before Melissa could answer her, the bell rang, signaling the end of lunch.

Relieved, Camille stopped swinging the rope mid-swing. It fell to the ground.

Melissa huffed. "How many was *that*?" she barked at Gabbie. Gabbie was daydreaming about the mural contest, not counting jumps. Melissa's eyes narrowed. "Weren't you counting?"

Gabbie swallowed. Her heart banged in her chest. "Ah, yes, I *was*," she said nervously. She looked at me hoping I could help her out.

Three hundred twelve, I said. Gabbie repeated it to Melissa. "It was definitely three hundred and twelve. I'm certain of it."

"*Drats*! I only had a few more jumps! Tomorrow, you'll have to skip eating altogether if I'm to break my own record." She raised her brows. "Do you have a problem with that?"

Tell her yes! I said. *You and Camille deserve a chance to jump.* But instead, Gabbie and Camille nodded their heads in unison. Melissa grinned, victoriously. She stepped over the rope and marched towards the school building. When she was out of earshot, Camille told Gabbie she should have lied. "If you told her she broke her record, then maybe we would've had the chance to jump."

Gabbie sighed. She hadn't thought to lie.

As the girls walked across the courtyard, Gabbie stopped to tie her shoe. Before she stood back up, the clouds blew past the sun, and a shiny copper coin started to shimmer in the sunlight. "Hey look, a penny!" she said. She held it high to show Camille.

Melissa, who was standing in the doorway, turned to look. "What's with you and those stupid pennies?" she barked. Her lip sneered in disapproval as Gabbie tucked the coin into her skirt pocket. "That angel thing is just some stupid myth."

Camille, on the other hand, smiled widely and asked, "Is it from your mom?"

Gabbie withdrew the penny from her pocket and looked at the date. A smile stretched across her face. "Yup, it's from her."

"Are you sad?" Camille asked. Gabbie had once told her that her mom sent her pennies when she was sad.

Gabbie thought about it for a second. "Nope, not at the moment."

Chapter Six

The Masters

*A*s Gabbie lay in bed later that night, the moonlight shone through the window making everything in the room look blue. Her arms were tucked behind her head. "Why would someone cut off their own ear?" She asked.

It took me a minute to follow her train of thought. Then I remembered the slide show she watched in class today. She was referring to Vincent van Gogh. I stretched out at the foot of her bed. *Why don't you ask him?* I said.

"How?" Gabbie asked.

He's working on a new painting in the Temple of Artistic Endeavors. We can go there once you fall asleep, I said.

"Really?"

Of course, I said. *Just because he no longer lives on earth doesn't mean he no longer exists.*

She snapped her fingers. "That's right, I keep forgetting," she said apologetically.

Across the room, Victoria stirred in her bed. "Can't you talk to your imaginary friend in your head?" she grumbled.

"No," Gabbie grumbled back. "I can't. *And he's NOT imaginary!*"

This time it was me who snapped my fingers. *Why didn't I think of that?* I said.

"Think of *what?*" Gabbie asked.

Victoria huffed, took her pillow, and covered her head.

We can talk telepathically, I told Gabbie. *I have your chart, so I know where and what and why you do things, but I can't hear your thoughts. But if you give me permission to read your mind..."*

Gabbie interrupted. "Can't you do that already?"

No. Your thoughts are private, just between you and God and your angels. But if you let me read your mind, then we can talk, and no one could hear us.

"Then I won't look like a freak who talks to herself!" Gabbie said excitedly.

Victoria kicked her feet. "You *are* a freak! Just go to sleep already."

The deal was struck. Gabbie allowed me to enter her head. *Now, think of something,* I said.

Like what? She asked, just using her mind.

I laughed. *It worked,* I told her. Her thoughts came through loud and clear.

It took only minutes for me to regret our new arrangement. Gabbie's brain never stopped. She thought about the mural contest. She thought how cool it was talk to me whenever she wanted. She thought of the mural contest. She thought of me. The mural contest. Me again. And then a random thought about Noel. I wasn't ready for that. And neither was she. She tossed it out as soon as it came in and replaced it with me. Then the contest. Then me.

It took more than two hours before Gabbie's brain stopped thinking. *Blah, blah, blah, blah,* is all I heard until she finally fell asleep. And as soon as she did, her soul popped out of her body and hovered over the bed.

"Whew, I thought I'd *never* fall asleep," she said. She tugged at the silver cord attached to her belly. It stretched and bounced back, nice and tight. She grabbed my hand and we rushed out the open window.

The sky was as dark as ink and spotted with brilliant twinkling stars. We soared through the night until the sky turned pink, and when it did, Gabbie smiled. She knew we had arrived.

We gently touched down in front of the *Temple of Artistic Endeavors.* Two huge columns framed the entrance of the octagon building and had several wings that jetted off the sides. We raced up the marble steps and past the giant Greek columns. The music playing throughout the hall was familiar to her. "Is that John Lennon?" she asked. He was one of her grandmother's favorite musicians.

"It sure is. He's been working with George Harrison on a couple of new tunes."

"Remind me tomorrow to tell Nana. She's going to flip out," Gabbie said excitedly.

The walls inside the temple were crowded with paintings, all of which graced museum walls *there.* Besides paintings, there were sculptures and jewels and artifacts. None of which were locked away. Gabbie tried on the Queen of England's crown and slipped inside King Tut's tomb. She tried on a pair of ruby red slippers and clicked her heels three times. A smile broke across Gabbie's face. "Dorothy was right, there is no place like home."

I guided her down the next hallway. When we stopped to look at the *Mona Lisa*, a man with frizzy hair and a long curly beard appeared magically by our side. He wore a big floppy hat with a small brim. A leather vest covered his torso, and the sleeves of his linen shirt were large and puffy. He wore wool stockings instead of pants and well-worn leather boots.

"Mr. da Vinci?" Gabbie gasped.

Leonardo took his hat from his head and bowed. "Pleased to make your acquaintance."

"Yes, it is," Gabbie said, nervously. She giggled when she realized what she had said. "I mean it's nice to meet you, *too.*"

Leonardo smiled. "Tell me, what do you think of her?" he asked, referring to his painting.

"I thought it would be bigger," Gabbie said honestly. The painting was of average size.

"What, like *that*?" asked a second voice in the same Italian accent as Leonardo's. Gabbie turned, her eyes wide. This man also had a long beard and was dressed in a brown tunic covered by a long black robe. She followed the man's finger. It pointed to a huge—and I mean *huge*—statue made from marble.

"That's the statue of David. We studied it in school," Gabbie said. She snapped her fingers and pointed at the second man. "So, that must mean you're Michelangelo."

Michelangelo bowed. "At your service, Madame."

"Is it true that he was already in the marble and all you had to do was chip him out?" Gabbie asked.

Michelangelo nodded. "I knew David was already created *here*," he said, running his hand down the length of the marble slab. "It took two years *there*, but I finally got him out."

By the time Claude Monet appeared, Gabbie was accustomed to the artist suddenly appearing by our side. Monet, like the others, wore a hat and had a long bushy beard. His wardrobe, unlike those of his counterparts, was more up to date. A wide necktie hung from his loose white shirt. He wore an overcoat and a pair of dark linen pants.

A gigantic painting of water lilies took up one entire wall. "You sure do love painting water lilies," Gabbie said.

Monet replied, "The subject is not important to me; what I want to reproduce is what exists between the subject and me."

I looked at Gabbie to see if she understood. Her head nodded as her fingers cupped her chin. I knew she didn't know what the heck he was saying, but she sure looked as if she did.

After taking in Monet's other masterpieces, we stopped to look at another famous painting. Swirls of color painted in small strokes filled the canvas.

"I can do that," Gabbie said as we looked at *The Starry Night*.

"Is that so, *Mon Cherie*?" asked a redheaded man. His words were drenched by a deep French accent.

Stunned, Gabbie just stared at the man. Her thoughts bounced around in her head. *One, two. A right one and a left one. This couldn't be him, could it? He has both his ears. A right one and a left one. One ear, two ears. But it looks like Vincent van Gogh. But it can't be. This man has both his ears.* Her thoughts bounced back and forth within her head. It was like watching a tennis match. One, two. One, two.

By the time she finally asked the question I was nearly dizzy. "I just thought you only had one ear. I mean … that's what they told me in school. That you cut off your own ear."

Vincent held his stomach while he laughed. "Oh yes, yes. Such a dreadful thing. I don't know what demon possessed me to do such a thing."

"You were possessed by *demons*?" Gabbie gasped. Fear exploded through her mind. *Demons? What kind of demons? Do they have red horns? And fangs? I bet they're really big! And pointy! Where do they live? Can they get me, too?*

I squeezed my hands to the side of my head. I didn't know how I was going to handle this. Listening to her every thought was starting to drive me insane.

Vincent furrowed his brows. He was totally confused. I told him Gabbie was on a class trip, that she was attending earth school and that she didn't remember all the ways of *here*. Vincent laughed again. "Oh, my dear, my demons were my own. Terrible things, really, the things your earthbound ego can create."

"So you *did* cut off your own ear then?" she asked.

"Yes, I did. But isn't it sad that with all the beauty I created, it's my pain and suffering that sticks out the most?" He laughed again. "Or, should I say, *didn't*." He circled his ear with his finger.

Gabbie's brows scrunched together. She didn't get his joke. I, on the other hand, thought it was hysterical. I slapped him on the back and we laughed. Monet, Michelangelo, van Gogh, and me.

Gabbie didn't think it was funny at all. She stomped her foot. "What's so funny?" she demanded.

Between my bursts of laughter, I was finally able to circle my finger around my ear. "His ear ... it didn't *stick out*." I held my stomach. I was laughing so hard I was getting a pain in my side.

The joke still didn't make Gabbie laugh, even though I explained it to her. She stood with her hands on her hips and said, "I don't that's very funny."

Vincent smiled. "Never mind, Mon Cherie. Tell me, do you like to paint?"

I tried to muffle my laugh as Gabbie nodded her head. "I do, but at the moment I'm stuck. I want to win the mural contest at school. The theme this year is self-empowerment and I have no idea what to paint."

Vincent scratched his chin. "Maybe I can be of assistance to you."

"Could you, I mean, *would you* help me?" Gabbie asked excitedly.

"Of course, of course," Vincent said.

Leonardo chimed in. "We can *all* help."

Michelangelo agreed. "We've helped many souls in earth school," he said.

Gabbie wrapped her arms around Vincent and gave him a big squeeze. "Now I'm *sure* to win the contest. When do we begin?"

The masters huddled together to discuss when would be a good time and decided on the following afternoon, right after Gabbie got out of school. Together they would teach her all she needed to know in order to win the mural contest.

Gabbie couldn't get back to her body fast enough. She yanked on the silver cord. Within seconds, she flew out of the *Temple of Artistic Endeavors*. Instead of taking in the sights, she went directly home. She passed through the wall between dimensions and headed straight toward her rooftop. She was flying so fast she was out of control. Her hair whipped around her head obscuring her view. Her arms waved in circles. Her legs kicked helplessly as if she were caught in a riptide. I knew if she didn't recover control by the time she fell through the attic, her soul would miss her body altogether. And if that happened there was no telling how long it would take until her body let her soul in.

I took off after her. I had to get her back on track. But when I tried to help, she swatted at my hand. "I can do it myself," she said impatiently.

I backed off. "Suit yourself," I said.

As I predicted, Gabbie's soul missed her body—though I must admit she came closer than I thought she would. Her soul bounced next to her body still sleeping on the bed. She glared at me. "Don't even think about telling me *I told you so*."

"I'm only here to help you," I said. "But as long as you ignore my advice ..."

She held up her hand, palm facing toward me. "I know, I know, I'll suffer unnecessarily."

With a grunt of frustration, she flopped back on bed. "So, what do I now?"

"Try giving your shell a poke," I said, taking a seat next to her.

She did.

No luck.

She brushed the hair off her face and traced the freckles making up her birthmark. She ran her finger along her lash line and blew into her ear. Her body reacted with a flinch, but still no luck. Her soul was still sitting on the edge of the bed, annoying her shell on purpose.

Victoria was up, her bed was made, and she was dressed. The clock read 7:42 a.m. Gabbie had only three minutes before the alarm would ring. She sprang to her feet and started jumping on the bed. "Come on already!" she said.

All of a sudden the silver cord jerked. With a jolt, her soul plunged into her body with only a minute to spare.

When the alarm rang, Gabbie slept right through it.

When it rang for the third time, Victoria pulled the covers off her sister, picked up her tousled blonde hair, and blew the whistle directly into her ear.

Gabbie sprang up. "I'm up," she said, still half asleep.

Victoria huffed. "It's about time." She put the whistle back on her dresser and left the room.

Visions of last night's adventure flashed through Gabbie's mind. She whipped off the covers. They fell to the floor. "Victoria, wait!" she yelled, jumping out of bed. "You're never going to believe who I met last night." She started to run toward the stairs, but her feet got tangled up in the sheet and she landed face first in one of her old tennis shoes. "Yuck!" she exclaimed. Her sneakers smelled like cheddar cheese. She blew air out her nose in short forceful blows trying to get the odor of smelly feet out of her nose.

After pulling on her uniform, she raced downstairs. It was terribly wrinkled, but she didn't care. The whole house rattled and clanked. Then a boom announced her arrival. Nana flinched and held her heart.

"Is that the way you're going to school?" Nana asked when Gabbie plowed into the kitchen.

"Yes," Gabbie said, taking the bowl from her grandmother's hand. She didn't know why she would ask such a silly question. It was the same white shirt and the same plaid skirt she wore every day except for weekends. Then she wore a pair of jeans and a pink T-shirt. Always pink. Some dark pink. Some light pink. But they were always pink. Pink, pink, pink. Just like the sky in heaven.

Victoria shook her head in disgust. "Your shirt's on inside out and your left sock's a quitter."

Gabbie looked down. "Hmm, how 'bout that." Yesterday her right sock had hung down around her ankle and today she found its mate.

The breakfast conversation was the same as most mornings. Gabbie talked about heaven, how she met the masters, and how she heard John Lennon singing a new song. Victoria rolled her eyes. Nana listened enthusiastically.

"Did you know all of earth's master pieces were created in heaven first? That is why so many of the buildings and works of art here so hard to explain. The ancient civilizations for example – like the Egyptians - were infused with architecture way beyond their scope of reality."

"Is that so?" Nana said, impressed.

Victoria rolled her eyes some more, which made me wonder; with all that eye movement it's a wonder she doesn't get dizzy.

When breakfast was over Nana read Gabbie's tealeaves. The prediction: *Prominent figures will come for a visit.*

Once again, Nana's interpretation of the little soggy brown speckles covering the bottom of the teacup was spot on. That day after school, four of the most influential painters who ever walked planet Earth would come to help Gabbie with her mural entry.

Chapter Seven
Inspiration

As Gabbie and her friends walked to school, a pair of dragonflies caught her attention. "Hey look," she said pointing up to the sky.

Camille looked up. "Are those the dragonflies?" They flew through the air, climbing and diving, spifnning and soaring.

Melissa didn't even sneak a peak. She kept her eyes on the sidewalk. She wasn't going to give them the satisfaction.

As the pair of dragonflies danced in the air twinkles of light floated down from the sky, just like snow. Gabbie stretched out her arms and began to twirl. Camille twirled too. Gabbie and Camille both laughed. Together they twirled and laughed and laughed and twirled until ... *bam!* Gabbie twirled right into the meanest girl in school.

"That's it!" Melissa shouted. She dropped her backpack and raised her fist. She shook it in Gabbie's face. Gabbie backed away cautiously. Camille backed away, too. "If you do one more thing to make me angry..." Melissa snarled, but she didn't have time to finish her threat. The sound of a crossing guard's whistle blared through the air.

Gabbie was glad. She didn't want to know what Melissa would do if she had the chance to do it.

I was just glad Melissa wasn't my responsibility. If she were, I'd probably be the first guide to quit.

The day passed without further incident. There was no twirling, no talk of pennies, and there was definitely no talk of me. But the dragonflies didn't fear Melissa's warning. They showed up exactly when the bell rang ending the school day.

Gabbie followed the dragonflies across 7th Avenue without pointing them out. She tried really hard not to watch them as they danced through the air. She tried really hard not to twirl when the twinkling light rained down from above. But what she couldn't ignore was the feeling growing inside her. The sadness—which had snuck into her soul without her knowing—came out of her body and grew into a smile.

Then, the blue dragonfly did the strangest thing. It buzzed around her head and stopped right in front of her face. Its wings fluttered so fast that Gabbie couldn't see them move. What she couldn't miss was the giant pair of blue eyes staring straight at her. Gabbie couldn't help but stare back. They were the most beautiful eyes she'd ever seen. They weren't bug's eyes. In fact, they looked more human, almost ... angelic.

And if that weren't strange enough, Gabbie could swear she heard the insect talk. But the words weren't spoken out loud. They were delivered straight into her head.

She tore her stare from the bug's eyes and looked at me. *Was that you?* She asked.

I shrugged. *Nope. Not me.*

Gabbie looked back at the dragonfly still hovering in the air. "Can you repeat that?" She asked, politely. She held her hand to her ear. Her head tilted to the side as she tried to grasp the message. The words *be true to yourself in your heart* circled around in her mind.

"What does *that* mean?" Gabbie asked, but the dragonfly didn't answer; it simply flew away. "Wait! Don't go!" she shouted. She turned quickly with hope of following it only to come face to face with Melissa.

Melissa used her height to intimate her. As she peered down at Gabbie, her eyes were beady, and her braces looked like razors wrapped around a giant set of fangs. "So now we're talking to bugs?" Melissa said, her cackle filling the air. "You're such a freak!"

Gabbie started to protest. "I... but she stopped. After all, she *was* talking to a dragonfly, which certainly made her look like a freak. How could she defend herself when what Melissa said was true?

Chapter Eight
Swoosh Goes the Paint

Mr. Fiddlydinks hissed and jumped off the stoop as Gabbie climbed the steps of the brownstone. When the front door slammed behind her, Victoria gasped. She was in the foyer picking up the mail. Some days the mail carrier pushed the mail through the slot in the front door so hard that it scattered across the foyer floor. This was one of those days.

"Sorry," Gabbie said. "I didn't mean to scare you." Gabbie dropped her backpack on the chair next to the staircase. It rolled off the chair and fell to the floor with a bang.

Victoria gasped again. "I swear, Gabbie, you could wake the dead," her sister grumbled.

Gabbie sighed as she slapped her hands against her legs in frustration. "How many times do I have to explain it? They're not really *dead*," she whined. She picked up her backpack and looked for a safer place to toss it. "They're more alive over *there* than they are here. Or is it here and we're there?" She shrugged and tossed her backpack on the sofa. It bounced a few times but this time it stayed put.

When Gabbie turned to make her way towards the kitchen, she stumbled over the edge of the area rug covering the living room floor. The antique wool rug had strings that hung from the edge. They drove Nana nuts if they weren't perfectly straight. She had a special rake that would comb them into place. and she used it every day, whether the strings were messy or not.

"Whoa," Gabbie grunted. She tried to regain her balance. Her arms swung in circles but she hit the floor anyway. The fibers of the antique carpet were thick and scratched the skin off the tip of her chin. She rolled over on her back, grabbed her chin, and kicked her feet. "Ouch, ouch, ouch," she cried.

Victoria shook her head. "You're such a drama queen."

Gabbie's feet stopped kicking. "How would you feel if your face was scraped with steel wool?" she hissed.

"For your information it's alpaca," her sister replied.

Gabbie crinkled her nose and waddled her head. "*It's alpaca*," she mumbled, mimicking her sister.

Hurried footsteps raced across the floor. When Nana Alice entered the living room, she was out of breath and her hand covered her heart. "What on *earth*?" she exclaimed when she saw Gabbie sprawled across the floor. "I swear child, one day you'll be the death of me," Nana mumbled to herself. But the implication was heard, loud and clear.

"I just tripped, that's all. I'm fine. I swear. Nothing to worry about," Gabbie said as she got to her feet. A bright red carpet burn graced her chin.

Armed with a giant bag of ice under her chin, as Gabbie climbed the stairs to her room she suddenly remembered she had a date. With all the to-do about her chin, it had slipped her mind. She raced up the steps. Boom, boom, boom, stumble, boom, boom, boom.

The easel Nana had found at a thrift store stood in the corner of the room. Gabbie squeezed fresh paint onto her pallet. She ripped off a clean piece of paper from her painting pad. She was ready for the masters. But after a few minutes of pacing and fingernail biting, she flopped onto the bed. "Why didn't they show up?" she asked me.

Victoria, who was reading on her bed, put the book down and glared at her. "Who are you talking about?"

With a wave of her hand, Gabbie said, "Never mind. It doesn't matter. None of it matters."

You have to ask them to come, I told her. *They won't come unless you ask them to come.*

Gabbie shot up. "What ... like vampires?" she shouted.

Victoria's lips curled in. She slapped the book down on the bed. "What on earth are you talking about?"

"Oh sorry. I'm not talking to you. I'm talking to Samuel," Gabbie said.

Victoria rolled her eyes. "I'm really starting to worry about you," she said before going back to her book.

You would think she would be used to me talking to you by now, Gabbie said silently to me.

I agreed.

So tell me, what do I have to say to get the masters here?
I shrugged. *Just ask.*

Gabbie closed her eyes. Why? I have no idea. But if I were to guess, I would say she thought it held some special power. It didn't.

Okay you master guys, you can come anytime now! Gabbie said.

She waited a few seconds before peeling one eye open. When she did, there standing next to her were Michelangelo, Leonardo, Vincent, and Monet.

"Wow! Thanks for coming," she said excitedly.

Victoria didn't roll her eyes this time. She was too interested in her book. It was about a boy who falls in love with a girl in another dimension. I thought it was quite ironic how she could wonder if that could actually happen and at the same time not believe in me.

Gabbie stared at the stark white paper hanging from the clips on the easel. "I have no idea where to begin," she said.

Michelangelo said, "The masterpiece is already there— all you have to do is ask and it will be revealed."

Gabbie snapped her fingers. "That's right. I'll ask God for help."

After she prayed, she picked up the paintbrush and dipped it into the paint. "Just let it flow," Michelangelo said. She took a deep breath and touched the brush to the paper. It was Monet who instructed her first. Together they created the background rich with deep purples and blues. Leonardo helped with the dragonflies. One green. One blue. Vincent helped with the tiny flecks of gold paint that turned into words.

When the painting was done, Gabbie couldn't believe her eyes. All the other paintings she had done before this one lacked something special. They were ordinary, but not this one. This painting was truly magnificent, better than anything she'd ever painted before.

There was something familiar about the saying: *Be true to yourself in your heart.* But she couldn't quite place it. She tapped her finger on her chin. Then her eyes grew wide. "Hey, wait a minute!" she said. Wasn't that what the dragonfly said when it hovered in front of her face as she walked home from school?

I nodded my head. *Pretty cool, huh?*

Chapter Nine
A Deeper Meaning

But I still don't know what it means, Gabbie said.

I suggested she look in a book Nana kept in the study.

The fastest way down to the study was via the banister. She hoisted her leg over the staircase railing. The last time she slid down the banister she had lost her balance, tipped to the outside, and hung by her fingertips, three stories high. That way the reason Nana started practicing yoga. It had taken Nana and Victoria ten whole minutes to tie a rope around her waist and hoist her to safety. Then she spent the next few hours in the emergency room. Not from her own injuries—a minor rope burn around her waist—but because of Nana's heart. It began to race uncontrollably. That's when she had made a promise to God. She told him she would never slide down the banister again if he didn't take her Nana. Nana told her it didn't work that way, so one quick ride down the railing shouldn't make much difference. Besides, she was older now and had better balance.

Luckily for both her, and Nana, she traveled down the banister without incident, unless you count her dismount. When she got to the bottom of the staircase, she had built up so much speed that her fingers couldn't squeeze the railing tight enough to stop her downward motion. She slammed to the floor with a bam. The windows rattled. The figurines in the curio wiggled, and the silver platter, which leaned against the glass, slid down a bit. Thankfully, the crystal clock stopped it from sliding all the way down, taking everything on the shelf with it.

"Sorry!" Gabbie shouted before Nana could scold her. She tore down the hallway and slid sideways into the library. Nana Alice had a huge collection of books. There were shelves of books she still hadn't read yet. That's what she planned on doing when she retired, but now she was lucky if she got through one chapter before falling fast asleep. She didn't complain though. She said one day when the girls are grown there would be plenty of time to read.

Gabbie skimmed her finger along a shelf. Halfway through, I pointed to a book with a purple spine. She pulled the book from its resting place. *The Complete Guide to Animal Spirits and Totems.*

She thumbed through the pages until she found the word *dragonfly*. Her eyes zoomed in on the description. "It says here that dragonflies are associated with discovering one's true self."

Her eyebrows scrunched together for a moment but sprung up again the second she understood the meaning. "Oh, I get it! It means that no matter what, it's important to be yourself. Don't change for anyone." She snapped the book shut. "I think it's perfect for my mural entry," she said. "Every morning when the kids come into school it will remind them to be themselves. Don't try to be someone they're not."

A smile stretched across my whole face. *I think it's perfect, too.* But there's one more thing she had to discover. So, I sent her a thought.

The second it popped into her head, it popped out of her mouth. "Do you think there's a reason why the dragonflies are different colors? Why one is blue and the other one green?"

Good question, I said.

The computer where Gabbie and Victoria completed their homework sat on top of the desk facing the bay window. It took a few minutes for the machine to wake up, and when it finally did, Gabbie typed *meanings of colors* into the search engine.

A whole slew of entries popped up. I pointed to a color chart and Gabbie clicked on it.

I thought I might have to explain how the colors translated to the dragonflies, but to my delight Gabbie understood. "The green dragonfly represents safety ... and the blue dragonfly, trust. So, I guess it means it's safe to trust myself."

A smile spread across her face and I was so glad she understood. I hoped she'd remember it when she was put to the test.

Chapter Ten

Pennies

The following morning, Gabbie inched her way down the stairs, painting in hand. It was the first time since she had moved into her grandmother's house that the windows didn't rattle, or the plates didn't shake. The silverware was silent and the crystal clock was safe. She didn't want to take a chance on anything happening to her masterpiece. It was the last day to enter the mural contest, and if anything happened to her entry it would be too late to paint another one.

"Ta-da!," Gabbie sang as she entered the kitchen. She held up her painting with a smile so big it showed every tooth in her mouth.

Nana gasped. She hadn't heard Gabbie coming. Once she calmed her heart down, she asked, "Is that your entry for the mural contest?" Her eyes widened as she looked at Gabbie's painting.

"Yup. What do you think?" Gabbie asked proudly.

"It's terrific!" Nana said excitedly. She clapped her hands. "I have a good feeling about this. Oh it's good. I can *feel* it!" She pointed to her stomach. "Right here ... in the middle of my solar plexus." When Nana had that feeling, she was never wrong.

Gabbie giggled then bowed. "I accept this award, thank you God. Thank you for letting me win the mural contest."

Victoria walked into the kitchen. "You won the mural contest?" she asked, surprised. "I thought the winner wasn't going to be announced until next week!"

"I'm just thanking God in advance," Gabbie said. "As if it already happened."

Victoria rolled her eyes. "I don't think it's a good idea to get your hopes up," she said.

Nana gasped. "We need to put it out there. Reach for the stars. Dream big. Dream huge. And thank God as if it already happened!" Nana exclaimed.

All I could *hope* for was that the next part of the plan goes smoothly because if it doesn't, things could get totally out of hand.

Carefully, Nana rolled up the painting and slid it into the cardboard cylinder she had picked up at the post office. Gabbie grabbed her backpack and then tucked the cylinder protectively under her arm. Nana kissed her on the cheek and wished her luck. Gabbie ran her hand over her stomach. "There's so many butterflies flying around in my belly that if I opened my mouth wide enough they might come fluttering out."

Victoria followed her sister outside. "Good luck," she said as she skipped down the porch steps. "I *hope* you win."

The morning sun filtered between the skyscrapers, creating long shadows in the street. Melissa's shadow was stretched all the way across the street. It tapped one of its giant feet.

"Is that your entry?" Melissa growled. Her face was scrunched up on one side. Camille however, squealed with excitement. "Yeah! You finally did it."

Gabbie nodded. "I finished it last night."

"Can I see it?" Camille asked.

Melissa didn't wait for Gabbie to answer her. "We'll be late," she snapped. She took Camille by the arm and pulled her down the sidewalk.

I was glad. I worried that if Gabbie took the picture from the cylinder, something (or someone) might "accidentally" ruin it on purpose.

As the girls made their way down the avenue, Gabbie spotted something shiny in the street. She bent down to take a closer look.

Camille crouched down next to her. "Is that what I think it is?"

"Yup," Gabbie said excitedly. She carefully plucked the penny—which was balancing precariously on the edge of the sewer grate—checked the date, smiled, and stuck it in her pocket.

Melissa stood on the curb; her face was red with anger. "What's with you and those stupid pennies?"

Camille pushed her glasses up the bridge of her nose. "Her mom sends them to her."

Melissa crumpled her lip in disapproval. "Your mother can't send pennies from heaven. She's dead." She hoisted her backpack over her shoulder and marched off, chin high.

"No she's not!" Gabbie shouted. "She just lives in another dimension."

I wrapped my arm around her shoulder and gave it a squeeze. She couldn't feel it of course, but I did nonetheless.

I was proud of her. Maybe now, what's to come won't be as bad as I was starting to believe it could be.

The day was like every other day. There was math, science, language studies, and tons of random thoughts. I ran my fingers through my wavy blonde hair tugging madly at the strands. This is why guides didn't crawl into their responsibilities' heads. Gabbie's mind bounced from one subject to another. One second she was thinking about how cool the colors painted on her pencil looked as she rolled it on her desk, and the next second she was wondering how long Mrs. Jones's hair was. Every day her teacher wore her hair in a bun, and Gabbie didn't know if it touched her shoulders or her waist. She wondered what it would be like to have hair as long as Rapunzel's. A chill ran down her arms as she pictured herself locked away in a tower. I'd hate to be locked in a tower. What if it were so high Prince Charming couldn't climb it? Then I'd be stuck there until I died. And that would stink. It had been less than a day and I already had a major headache.

There has got to be a way to filter what she's thinking so I don't have to listen to this nonsense, I thought—and just as I did, *The Spirit Guide Handbook* appeared in my hand.

I love the law of attraction. *Here* anything we desired magically appeared.

I flipped to the help section. I found what I was looking for under *Filters.* According to the handbook, I could place a filter over my head, allowing only pertinent information through.

One thought later, I was in possession of a mind filter. It looked similar to one of those coffee filters Nana used every morning in the automatic coffee machine. I took the filter, which was made of a silk-like substance, and placed it over my head. I sighed with relief. It worked. All the unimportant gibberish that Gabbie was thinking instantly disappeared.

After the morning lesson, there was lunch and recess, where there was a lot of rope turning, but no jumping—at least not for Gabbie or Camille. But, that didn't matter to Gabbie. She was too preoccupied with the mural contest and her amazing entry to care whether she got a chance to jump or not.

"You could win, you know," Camille whispered as they walked home from school. "And if you did, I bet Melissa would be piping mad. She probably won't let you jump at lunch anymore."

"She doesn't let us jump now," Gabbie reminded her.

Camille agreed.

"Besides, if I did win, I won't be at lunch; I'll be painting the mural," Gabbie said hopefully.

Camille giggled. "That would make her even madder. Who would turn the rope if you aren't there to do it?"

Gabbie shrugged her shoulders. She really didn't care. All she cared about was winning the mural contest.

"I'm home," Gabbie shouted. She threw her backpack on the chair next to the front door and ran up the stairs, two at a time. She hurried to her chest of drawers. She kept all her pennies in an old mason jar. Nana had tons of them stored in a box in the basement.

Gabbie took the jar and spilled the coins onto the dresser. From her pocket, she pulled out two more. She had found the first penny on the way to school and the second on the way home. It had been stuck in the crack of the sidewalk.

She counted the pennies twice just to make sure. "Thirty-four," she said proudly.

"What are you going to do with those?" Victoria asked, startling Gabbie. Gabbie jumped, letting go of the jar. Victoria reached over and grabbed the jar before it hit the floor.

"Don't do that!" Gabbie exclaimed. Her face scrunched up, her fists clenched. She hated when her sister snuck up on her.

"Do what?" Victoria replied, handing the jar back to her sister.

"Sneak up on a person," Gabbie huffed.

"Not everyone bounds up the stairs like a herd of elephants," Victoria said. She flopped down on her bed. "So ... how did it go today?"

"Great," Gabbie said. "Mama sent me two pennies." She held up the coins to show her sister. "And they all have Mama's birthday date on them."

"That's just a coincidence," Victoria said with a bite in her tone.

Gabbie put her hands on her hips and leaned toward her. "I can't talk to her during the day. Only at night, when I fly." Her tone was just as sarcastic as her sister's. "She sends me these, so I know she's with me."

Victoria didn't bother to reply. She just picked up her book—the one about the boy in another dimension—and began to read.

Gabbie scooped the pennies into her hand and dropped them in the jar. "Thanks, Mama." She turned and looked back at her sister. "I really think I'm going to win."

Chapter Eleven
The Announcement

The following morning, as soon as the alarm clock sounded, Gabbie threw off the covers and jumped out of bed. I had never seen her this excited. Today the results of the mural contest were going to be announced and she didn't want to be late.

She dressed, combed her hair, brushed her teeth, and raced down the stairs taking two steps at a time. In all her excitement, her foot slipped off a step, and the next thing I knew she was tumbling down the last few steps.

Crash!

Rattle!

Bang!

"Gabbie? Are you all right?" Nana shouted. Her voice was high and tight with fear.

Gabbie jumped to her feet and checked her extremities for damage. "I'm okay. Everything's fine," she said, and strolled into the kitchen hoping to pass off her fall as if nothing had happened.

Nana stood by the stove clutching her heart. "You must stop jumping down the stairs!"

Gabbie started to argue. "I didn't jump, I ..." But she stopped before she told Nana the truth. She'd rather have her think she jumped down the stairs than for her to know she fell. That was sure to make her heart stop beating.

Gabbie ate her oatmeal as quickly as she could and gulped down her tea. When she was finished she let out an enormous burp. "S'cuse me!" she giggled, wiping her mouth with the back of her hand.

Nana Alice shook her head in dismay. "I hope you don't do that in public."

"Nope," Gabbie said. "Only here."

The cuckoo clock began to chime. Gabbie shoveled the rest of her oatmeal into her mouth. "I gotta go," she said. "I don't want to miss the announcement." With a quick jerk she pushed herself from the table. Her elbow hit her teacup, sending it crashing to the floor. It shattered on impact, spilling its contents across the kitchen floor.

"Oh dear," Nana said.

Gabbie reached for a broken piece of china as tears formed in her eyes. "I'm sorry," she said. She knew how much her grandmother loved her blue willow china.

Nana grabbed for her hand but her voice was gentle. "It's only a teacup. Nothing to get worked up about. Besides, I have tons of them." She kissed Gabbie's forehead. "Now go. I'll get it. You have a contest to win."

The really cool thing about being a spirit guide is that I could bi-locate. In other words, I could be in more than one place at a time. As I walked with Gabbie to the front stoop, I hung out with Nana as she bent down to wipe up the tea spilled on the to wipe up the tea spilled on the kitchen floor.

I was curious to see what message spirit would leave in the tealeaves.

The tealeaves started to move, as if an unseen force was guiding them. Nana watched as the shapes started to come together. First a crown appeared. Nana smiled. She knew that a crown meant an impending victory. But her smile quickly faded. Next to crown the leaves formed a perfect teardrop.

Gabbie stood on her tippy-toes looking down the busy New York City street. Children laughed as they made their way to school. But Gabbie wasn't laughing as she waited on the stoop; she was way too nervous to laugh.

Normally, Melissa and Camille would be waiting for her, but today the stoop was empty, except for Mr. Fiddlydinks. He took off running the minute Gabbie came through the door.

She climbed the concrete wall separating the stoops, hoping to get a better view down the street. The sidewalk was crowded with pedestrians, but her friends were nowhere in sight. She thought, *Of all days to be late, why did it have to be today?*

The neighbor's door swung open. Gabbie hopped off the wall and shrank down behind it. Mr. WarsInski mumbled as he examined the stoop, looking for something, anything out of place. Once satisfied, he adjusted his hat and set off down the steps.

"What on earth are you doing?" Victoria asked, startling her sister.

Gabbie, who was pressed against the concrete wall, gasped and fell backwards onto her bottom. "Urgh," she mumbled. She hadn't noticed her sister standing next to her. The glass window in the front door hadn't rattled the way it did when she closed the door. It never did when Victoria was in charge.

"I'm hiding from old Mr. Warsinski. If he sees me, he'll find something to blame me for," Gabbie said.

"Well, you can get up now. He's gone," Victoria told her.

Gabbie sprang to her feet and straightened out her uniform. Today, her socks matched; neither one was a quitter.

"Good luck today," Victoria said. Her thick auburn hair bounced as she made her way down the stone steps.

"Thanks," Gabbie yelled, holding her fingers crossed. Within seconds, Victoria disappeared into the morning rush.

Gabbie glanced at her watch. Her heart started to beat really fast. She had only twelve minutes to get to school. Only twelve minutes before the announcement. She sighed with relief when her friends rounded the corner. Melissa didn't slow her pace as she approached the stoop. She had no intention of stopping to make small talk. It was obvious she was in as much of a hurry to get to school as Gabbie was.

"Let's go!" Melissa barked. Her eyes never left the sidewalk as her arms flailed by her sides.

Gabbie jumped from the stoop. Her backpack slipped, but she didn't stop to fix it. With a grunt, she hoisted it back into position.

Camille huffed as she tried to keep pace. "Hey, Gabbie, wait."

Gabbie did.

"Here," Camille said dropping the penny she found into Gabbie's palm. "I want you to have this. For good luck." Before Gabbie could thank her, a bright light shot up from the palm of her hand. Gabbie gasped. Camille shouted, "Did you see that?"

Melissa stopped mid-step. She turned around slowly, her eyes burning red. "See *what?*" she snarled. "It better not be another penny!"

"Ah? ..." Camille's eyes were huge as she looked at Gabbie for assistance.

Gabbie shrugged her shoulders. "I didn't see anything," she said innocently.

Thankfully, Melissa didn't care enough to ask anymore questions.

The whole school was buzzing with excitement. The entries for the mural contest were displayed in the main entrance for all the students to see. In the past, it was the students who voted for their favorite entry, but there was too much ballot stuffing, so the art teacher decided it was only fair to have the teachers vote. No names were attached to the entry, only a number. Each teacher would then choose what painting best captured the contest's theme. This year the theme was self-empowerment.

I walked with Gabbie as she looked over each entry. Her heart started racing. Her nerves were getting the better of her.

Just relax, I told her.

How am I supposed to relax? she answered. *All of these paintings are so much better than mine.*

You're being too hard on yourself. True, each painting is different, but your painting is just as good as any of these, I said.

She chewed on her bottom lip and picked at her fingers as she stared at each entry. But it was Noel's drawing that made her shoulders slump. She sighed. *This is really good,* she told me.

She was right. Noel's entry was really good. A boy sat on top of a pile of books. "Knowledge is Power," was written in a banner above his head.

Next to Noel's painting was Gabbie's. Its simple message spoke volumes. *Be true to yourself in your heart.* Nothing could be more empowering than being you. Gabbie stood for a moment taking it in. I placed my hand in hers.

We made our way down the hall, taking in the remaining entries. Melissa stood in front of the last painting with a smile plastered across her face. Something green twisted around the wires in her mouth.

"They saved the best for last," Melissa said. Gabbie gagged. I wasn't sure if it was because of her nerves, Melissa's entry or the green thing between her teeth.

If Gabbie's painting spoke volumes, Melissa's recited the whole library. Her painting consisted of a pile of children, one on top of the other. Their tongues were hanging out, and a girl who looked a lot like the artist was standing at the top of the heap. Her hands were clasped together in a victorious grip above her head. The banner read: *The Ladder of Success.*

Inside the classroom "Team Noel" rallied around his desk. His friends were excited. They were patting him on the back, sure he was the winner.

Gabbie squeezed between the boys and took her seat behind them. She picked at her fingernails, lost in worry. She didn't notice Camille standing next to her desk until she waved her hand in front of her face. "Hello, anybody home?" Camille asked.

Gabbie blinked several times, bringing her back to the present moment. "Huh?" she said.

Camille bent down and whispered into Gabbie's ear. She didn't want Melissa—who had just sat down at her desk—to hear her wish Gabbie luck.

Last year, when Lucy Martin had won the contest, Melissa slugged Camille in the arm when she heard Camille say congratulations. Camille wore a giant bruise for the next three weeks.

The clock read eight-thirty. At any minute the loudspeaker would crackle to life announcing the winner of the mural contest. Gabbie reached inside her pocket and pulled out the penny Camille had given her. She held it to her heart. No sooner had she sent up her prayer than Katherine appeared by my side.

"I don't think this is a good idea," I told her. "Maybe you should leave."

"Why?" she asked. But before I could tell her, the loudspeaker squawked to life. Gabbie drew in a deep breath as the announcer's voice cut through the air.

"Good morning, students." The voice belonged to Principal Ward. "As you know, the mural contest is a tradition here at Saint Bernadette's and we would like to thank all the participants. Though there were many wonderful entries in this year's mural contest, the judges have come to a unanimous decision." The principal paused for a recorded drum roll. Gabbie could hardly breathe. If they didn't announce the winner soon she would have to borrow Camille's inhaler.

I think I was just as nervous as Gabbie. My heart started to race and my palms began to sweat. Not because of the impending announcement, I already knew who the winner was. It was because things were about to change. From this moment on, Gabbie's life will never be the same.

After the drum roll ended, Principal Ward continued, "It is my honor to announce this year's winner ... congratulations to ... Gabriella Flowers."

Cheers filled the classroom. Gabbie couldn't believe it. *I won?*

Chapter Twelve
B is for Bully

Katherine jumped with joy. "She did it!"

"Yes, it's wonderful. Now leave," I said. I didn't want her to witness what might happen next.

Noel turned around in his chair and looked at Gabbie. By the look on Gabbie's face, it was obvious she didn't know what to expect. Her brows disappeared completely beneath her bangs and her eyes were round like marbles. When he smiled at her she let out her breath.

Noel stuck out his hand. As an athlete, he had learned how to be a gracious loser. "Congratulations," he said. He grabbed Gabbie's hand and shook it up and down as if he were trying to tug it clean off her body. "When I saw your entry, I knew I didn't stand a chance."

"I really thought you were gonna win," she confessed.

Noel shrugged his shoulders. "No big deal," he said.

But it was a big deal and he and Gabbie both knew it.

Mrs. Jones clapped. "Well done, Gabbie."

"Everyone is so excited for her," Katherine said. "I wish she knew I was here."

"Send her a penny," I said.

She gasped and drew her finger up. "That's right, with all the excitement, I forgot."

The next thing I knew, a shiny copper coin was rolling around Gabbie's desk. I still don't know how she got those pennies to materialize just with a thought. I scrunched my face, trying with all my might to send a penny, too, but as usual nothing happened.

Gabbie snatched the penny right before it fell to the floor.

Camille clapped. She was so excited. "A penny from heaven!"

Gabbie's face didn't seem big enough for her smile. All her classmates took turns congratulating her. They shook her hand and patted her on the shoulder. They were all so happy for her. All except one.

When Gabbie's eyes met Melissa's, her face flushed from rosy pink to pale white, as if someone had pulled a plug and all her blood had drained from her head. Melissa didn't shake her hand, pat her on the shoulder, or wish her well. She did, however, squint her beady little eyes and curl her upper lip. This, I knew, wasn't going to be good.

Dean took the huge megaphone—which he now kept with him—and held it to Melissa's ear. "Congratulate her!" His voice blasted into her head like an air horn. But there was no sign that it had registered at all. "I swear every time I give her advice she does the complete opposite, sending herself down a long a very bumpy path. I'm starting to get motion sickness," he said.

Instead of taking her guide's advice, Melissa stood with her hands curled up at her sides. Her nostrils flared so wide they took up half her face.

I was right. This wasn't going to be good.

Dean flipped frantically through the *The Spirit Guide Handbook* searching for something that would stop what I knew was about to happen. Katherine looked at me, her face stricken with worry. She grabbed my arm, her fingers tight around my bicep. "What's going to happen?" she said.

According to Gabbie's chart, there were two ways this could work out, one being easy and the other—well, let's just say Dean wouldn't be the only one headed down a bumpy road.

Dean tried again to get through to Melissa. He shouted so loud I was sure his voice would not only break through the wall between them, but all the windows as well. "Please Melissa. Take the high road. Be a good sport!" But she didn't seem to hear her guide, and if she did she didn't care to listen.

Gabbie tried to apologize. She rubbed her stomach. "I'm sorry," she said in a low squeaky voice, but the damage was already done.

Katherine rushed to her daughter's side. She placed her hand on her shoulder. "Don't be sorry, sweetheart. You won fair and square."

Gabbie turned and faced the front of the room as the pains in her belly grew. *What have I done?* she wondered.

You're fine. Everything is fine, I told her as fear raised my voice. My words were hurried. *Stay calm.* Heck, I needed to stay calm. I tried to convince myself that she was going to sail through this experience, but now, I'm not so sure.

I watched as Melissa pulled back her foot, preparing to give Gabbie's chair a swift kick.

Katherine gasped. "Hey, don't do that." She looked at Dean, panic screaming across her face. "Make her stop!"

Dean tried one more time to get through to Melissa, but when her lips curled, he knew what path she had chosen.

I closed my eyes. I knew what was coming and there was nothing Dean or I could do.

Bam! Melissa kicked the back of Gabbie's chair. Gabbie lurched forward. She had no idea what hit her.

"Stop!" Katherine cried.

Mildred covered her mouth. She was speechless.

Katherine turned to me for help. She gasped. "What's happening to you?" she asked.

"What do you mean?" I said. I had no idea what she was talking about.

"You're starting to fade." Her voice was trembling.

Now it was my turn to panic. I looked down at my hands. Instead of being opaque, they now looked a bit transparent. "I don't know." My voice was as shaky as hers.

It was Dean who explained. Apparently, Gabbie's fear was making me disappear. "Once you're totally invisible, she won't be able to communicate with you. You'll have to rely on sending advice through dreams and intuition. Just like the rest of us."

"I don't understand. I can see you, and Mildred, and Collette."

"Yes, you can see us, but Gabbie can't and soon she won't see you."

"It happened to me," Mildred said. "When Camille was one, I was solid as a rock. But I started to fade after that until, poof! I was gone."

I never noticed it before, but all the other spirit guides in the room had a subtle shimmery glow. I just assumed I did, too. But now I've learned that shimmery glow is more than an indication of our being, it's a death sentence.

If I didn't get Gabbie to calm down—and fast—the wall between us would start to thicken. And if it did, I would disappear and end up like Dean, and all the other guides in the room.

Again Gabbie tried to apologize. "I'm sorry," she said as tears appeared in her eyes. She didn't know what else to do. The pains in her belly circled like buzzing bees. *How in the world am I going to fix this?* She wondered.

"You don't need to be sorry, Gabriella." Her mother was as frantic as her daughter.

But, not as frantic as I was.

Melissa was growling at Gabbie. The green thing stuck in her braces wiggled. Her stringy brown hair draped across the sides of her cheeks. "Oh, you'll be sorry all right, cry baby." She kicked Gabbie's chair again, making sure she got the message.

My heart was beating so fast, I could hear it. *Thump. thump, thump.* If Gabbie didn't raise her hand and ask Mrs. Jones for help, I could be a shade lighter in a matter of seconds.

"Come on Melissa. Please, *stop!*" Gabbie pleaded. She tried to move her chair, but Melissa wouldn't let her. Her long skinny foot held Gabbie tight against her desk, cutting off her circulation. "Please let go. I can't breathe."

And neither could I. *Gabbie, listen to me. You have to stand up for yourself.*

She shook her head. *I not tattling, that will make things worse.* She was too strong, too stubborn, too thick headed, and in the end she won.

Melissa cackled. "Poor, poor crybaby," she said sarcastically. Before she took her foot away she gave one last nudge.

"Urgh," Gabbie sighed. I looked to Dean. "There must be something we can do."

While Dean searched through the handbook, Melissa searched her desk. A smile drew across her lips. She found what she was looking for. Dean didn't. He dropped the handbook and picked up the megaphone. Melissa checked to make sure Mrs. Jones wasn't looking. She wasn't. Her back was to the class as she wrote the next assignment on the blackboard. Melissa pulled the rubber band tight between her fingers. She took aim. Dean tried again to reach her, but like before he failed.

Pop! The rubber band snapped the back of Gabbie's head. "Ouch!" she shouted.

"Please, Samuel, you have to do something," Katherine begged.

I tried to get Gabbie's attention. I waved my arms in front of her face, but she just looked right through me. I jumped on the teacher's desk, calling out to her. *Gabbie! Tell her!* I said, waving my arms frantically. *Tell Mrs. Jones Melissa's kicking your chair and snapping rubber bands on the back of your head!* But it was no use. Gabbie's fear was screaming louder than I was.

Mildred tried to help. She whispered in Camille's ear. Camille raised her hand, but Melissa glared at her so she tucked it back on her lap obediently.

Plopping down on the edge of Mrs. Jones's desk, I resigned myself to Gabbie's choice. She could have spoken up, ending this fiasco before it progressed any further.

I unrolled Gabbie's scroll. There was no doubt about it. We just took a detour off a nice smooth highway unto a bumpy side road.

Lunch. Gabbie just knew it would be a nightmare. And so did I. Luckily she was to start the mural today. But Ms. Viotto, the art teacher, was in a meeting, so she couldn't go over the list of supplies until the end of the day.

What am I going to do?" she asked.

I pointed to my chest, which was a bit more lucent. "Me? Are you asking me?"

She swatted at me. When her hand passed through my arm, it made my skin crawl. Tiny shocks of electricity buzzed all the way to my shoulder. "Yikes! That's smart."

She wiggled her fingers at me. "Don't make me do it again."

"Alright, how about the library?" I suggested. This time, she took my advice. I thought I might regain some color, but to dismay I didn't.

Gabbie pulled the library door open. She peaked her head into the room hoping the librarian wasn't standing at the front desk. If she were, Gabbie would have to go back to the lunchroom. Food wasn't permitted in the library. But Gabbie didn't plan on eating. Her stomach was full. Full of nerves. Even her favorite sandwich-peanut butter and jelly sandwich wouldn't fit inside.

Gabbie was in luck. The librarian was nowhere in sight. She ran down the first aisle. A-F

There was a book cart at the end of the aisle. She positioned it so she could safely hide behind it. Even if the Librarian were to walk down the aisle, she wouldn't see Gabbie unless she moved the cart.

I took a seat on top of the cart and rested my chin on my fist. As I looked down at Gabbie, I wished there was some way I could fix this mess. Truthfully, I never expected the plan to take this turn. I really thought after the first kick Gabbie would have stood up for herself. It just goes to show you, when the green monster starts to stalk you, no telling how you might react. If it were up to me I would have warned her that this could happen. Then she would have been prepared. But it's against the rules. So instead of coming up with a plan, we're hiding in the library behind a book cart waiting for the bell to ring.

The torture continued through the afternoon lesson. *Bam, snap, kick.* Katherine sat next to Gabbie trying to soothe her daughter's nerves. She stroked her hand. "Please, sweetheart, tell the teacher what's going on." But it didn't do any good. Neither did the penny she dropped in her lap.

It was the longest day of Gabbie's life. When the bell finally rang, she grabbed her backpack and ran as fast as she could out of the classroom. She was supposed to check in with Ms. Viotto, to go over the list of supplies for the mural, but that was the last thing on her mind. All she wanted to do was to get home.

As Gabbie raced across 7th Avenue, she spotted the dragonflies overhead. I sighed with relief. If I couldn't get through to her, I knew that they could. Twinkles of light rained down from above, covering every inch of her like a blanket of love. Instantly, her dread vanished, and her pace slowed from a frantic rush to a light-hearted skip. Her fear was gone, at least for the moment.

Gabbie raced up the stoop, she was so excited to share the news. "I won! I won!" she yelled a she pushed her way through the front door. The plates on the cupboard clinked together as if celebrating her victory. She jumped and whooped, spinning round and round.

Nana raced through the brownstone to meet her. "What's this I hear?" she asked, her hand on her heart.

"I won! I won the contest," Gabbie sang, "I get to paint the mural! Woo-hoo!"

"That's wonderful!" Nana said, gathering her granddaughter in a hug. She had worried all day. Could the tear she saw in the tealeaves be a tear of joy?

"Tell me," Nana said, "What happened when you won?"

Nana Alice looked at Gabbie intently, hoping the tear was just that, a tear of joy.

I waved at Gabbie. *Tell her the truth. She can help you.*

But again, Gabbie chose a different path. "It was wonderful! Everyone one was so happy for me!"

I flopped down on the couch and covered my face with my hands (or what was left of them). The bumps had just turned into moguls.

Chapter Thirteen
Boy, What a Day

The following morning, Gabbie didn't want to get out of bed.

Come on sleepy head, you start the mural today, I said.

Memories from the day before, flooded her mind. She rubbed her belly. *I wish I never entered that stupid contest.* Then a thought popped into her mind and I wasn't the one who put it there. She snapped her fingers. "That's it!" she said excitedly. She jumped out of bed. She couldn't contain her excitement.

That's not going to solve your problem, I said as she hurried down the stairs. She had no intention of listening.

She gobbled down her breakfast, kissed her Nana, and raced out of the house. Mr. Fiddlydinks was napping on the stoop—that is, until the front door slammed.

"Meoooow!" he cried as he jumped to his feet. He hissed. But Gabbie didn't care. She wasn't going to waste one single second on that nasty old cat. She leaped from the stoop to the sidewalk. She threw her backpack over her shoulder and began to run.

Gabbie stood at the art room door. Her stomach flipped with anticipation. If all goes according to her plan, her troubles will soon be over.

"Can I help you with something dear?" Ms. Viotto asked. Fine grey hair popped out from beneath her blonde curly wig while several gold chains hung from her neck. Giant hoop earrings large enough for a bird to perch upon dangled from her ears and her dress was patterned with cats doing crazy things cats didn't do. Before Gabbie could tell her why she was there, Ms Viotto said, "Oh yes, supplies, supplies. You're starting the mural, so you need your supplies." The art teacher hurried to the back of the room where she pulled down a large box from the top shelf and raced back. "Here you go. I've already got everything you need to start, right here in this box." Her arms jangled with bracelets clear up to her elbows. She pushed the box toward Gabbie and guided her out of the classroom before Gabbie had the chance to speak.

"Wait, I have to talk to you," Gabbie said. She blocked the door from closing with the edge of her shoe.

Katherine appeared by my side. *Oh great.* "Please Katherine, leave," I said. Not only did I have to deal with Gabbie's fear; I had to deal with mother's too.

"I'm not going anywhere," Katherine said.

"It's not a request."

"If Gabbie is about to do what I think she's about to do, then she'll have to go through me," Katherine said. She pushed against the door, holding Gabbie back. The harder Gabbie tried to open the door, the more Katherine pushed back. I leaned against the wall, watching this exchange of willfulness. I shook my head as Katherine and Gabbie struggled to control the future.

Unwilling to give up her quest, Gabbie slammed her body hard against the door. The force was too much for Katherine to fight. The door flew open, sending Katherine through the air. Her arms flailed as she tried to maintain control. She sailed through the air and then through the art teacher's desk, landing silently on the floor. "Urgh," she said as she bounced to a stop. She blew her auburn hair from her forehead, amazed by her daughter's strong will.

Gabbie ran into the room. "Ms. Viotto, I think you made a mistake."

Katherine raced to the teacher's side. "Tell her you didn't," she pleaded.

By the look on the teacher's face, I knew she was confused. Her finger rested on her chin. "No, it's all there, everything you need," Ms. Viotto said.

"No, I mean the *contest*. I think you've made a mistake."

"Tell her she won fair and square," Katherine begged. "Don't let her quit. Please."

"There's no mistake, Gabbie. No other mural captured the meaning of self-empowerment as beautifully as yours did. It was unanimous. We loved everything about it. It was sheer genius. A true masterpiece," the art teacher said.

"But, but but..." Gabbie stuttered until she thought of her next move. "I ... cheated," she said. That should make her change her mind. "It wasn't me who really painted it."

"What?" Katherine gasped. I, however, knew this was coming. It said so in her chart.

"You didn't cheat. Anyone could ask heaven for help," Katherine said.

The teacher looked at Gabbie, brows raised. "If you didn't do the painting, Gabbie, then who did?"

Gabbie's eyes darted back and forth, searching for a lie. Lying wasn't her strong suit. And her mother knew it. She could always tell when her youngest daughter wasn't telling the truth. Her tongue grew thick and her words were sticky.

Katherine tapped her foot. "Well?" she said. She too wanted to be enlightened.

Gabbie swallowed, though it was difficult. She had hardly any moisture left in her mouth. "It was Leonardo," she managed to say.

Ms. Viotto's brows scrunched together. "Who? I don't know any student named Leonardo. Is he your brother? Your cousin? A neighbor?"

Gabbie shook her head. "No. It was Leonardo da Vinci. Michelangelo, Monet, and van Gogh helped too," Now that it was out of her head, she knew it sounded crazy.

The teacher laughed. "Yes. Yes, indeed. I did notice the similarities. Your choice of colors was no doubt inspired by Monet, and the brush strokes, clearly van Gogh."

"No," Gabbie said, holding her hands out to explain. "They *actually* helped. I held the brush, but they told me what to do. So, I just think you should award the mural to Melissa Graves. She paints way better than I do on my own."

The teacher tugged at her wig. "*Did* you or did you *not* paint that picture?"

Before Gabbie had the chance to answer, Katherine took her by the head and nodded it up and down. I cringed. She just interfered.

As if reading my mind she said, "Don't worry, I don't think it counts if I do it."

"Let's hope not," I said. I didn't tell her that if they pulled me, she's more than likely outta here too. I didn't want to have to deal with her worry too.

"Then it's settled. You won, fair and square," Ms. Viotto said. She then crawled beneath the desk, obviously in search of something.

"Did you see my box of chalk?" she asked. "I had it a second ago."

Gabbie joined the search. She crouched down on her knees and looked around the floor.

"Really, I want you to let Melissa paint the mural," she said as her eyes combed the floor tiles.

Katherine pushed a box of white chalk off Ms. Viotto's desk. To anyone who witnessed the act, it simply looked as if the box had lost its balance and tumbled to the floor. Then she wiggled a piece of chalk out of the box and sent it rolling across the floor. It stopped right under the teacher's nose.

"Oh, here it is," Ms. Viotto said, grabbing the chalk and sticking it in her bra. "Now," she huffed with relief. "What is it you need?"

"The mural, I think ..." Gabbie began to say, but before she could finish her sentence the teacher said no.

Katherine clapped excitedly.

"But, you don't understand ..." Gabbie said.

"I think I do. You want your friend to be happy. That's very nice, but you won hands down. It was unanimous. Now hurry along, hurry along. You're going to be late for class." Ms. Viotto waved her hand toward the door. "Now … what did I do with that chalk?"

Gabbie's plan tanked. *Now what am I going to do?* She thought. She rubbed her belly. The pains were back.

As we walked down the hallway, it was Katherine who noticed Melissa hiding in a classroom doorway. Her hand shook as she pointed towards the girl who made her little girl cry.

Look out! I shouted. It didn't do any good. Gabbie walked right by Melissa, lost in worry.

"I don't think she can hear you," Katherine cried.

There is only one way to find out if I was still being heard. I removed the filter, took a deep breath, and squeezed my eyes shut. If I was going to be certain, I had to go in.

The feeling of her blood rushed through me the second I stepped into her shell. The beat of her heart banged in my ears. It was so overwhelming that it was hard for me to hear my own thoughts. I fought the urge to fall out. *Come on, relax*, I told myself. *Just a few seconds is all I need.*

Gabbie! Gabbie! Can you hear me? I spoke directly into her mind hoping for a sign. A twitch. A flinch. A shudder. Anything to prove that I was still here. But all I heard was my own voice. It echoed through Gabbie's head as if I had shouted into an empty cavern.

Exhausted, I withdrew from her body. I was gone.

Katherine wrung her hands together. "So?" she asked.

I hated to tell her the news, but I couldn't lie, even if I wanted to. It went against everything I am. I shook my head. "It's not good," I said.

Katherine gasped. "You're glowing," she said.

We both knew why. Fear had finally taken Gabbie as its hostage. Until she surrendered and asked for help, there was nothing more I could do. What I did know was this: I had to ditch the filter, at least for now. I had to hear every thought, every fear, whether I liked it or not.

Dean shouted through his megaphone, but Melissa was determined to make Gabbie pay. She stepped into the corridor. Her lips were twisted white. She raised her arms, palms stretching out wide, and with all her might she shoved Gabbie as hard as she could from behind.

"*Urgh!*" Gabbie exclaimed. She lurched forward, losing her balance. The box of art supplies flew from her grip. It crashed on the floor with a bang. Tubes of paint rolled across the hall.

Melissa eyed a tube as it came to rest in front of one her really skinny feet.

"Don't!" Katherine shouted. But she, nor Dean, couldn't stop her.

Squish! Splat!

White paint exploded from the tube. It went through Katherine and landed all over Gabbie. It was in her hair, and on her face, and though it disappeared when it hit her blouse, it was there, too.

The all too familiar cackle filled the corridor. Melissa laughed so hard she couldn't breathe. Gabbie tried really hard to fight the tears. She bit her lip and squeezed her eyes tight. But her fear overwhelmed her. Tears rolled down her face. She had lost the fight.

"What's the matter, crybaby?" Melissa crowed.

"Do something, Samuel," Katherine begged.

I was at a loss. *Think, think, think.* Then something I read in *The Spirit Guide Handbook* popped into my head. *That's it,* I thought. *If I couldn't get through to Gabbie, maybe I could get someone else to help her.* I disappeared and then reappeared with Mrs. Jones by my side.

"What's going on here?" the teacher asked.

The look on Melissa's face turned from amusement into concern. "Gabbie had a little accident," Melissa replied. "She dropped her art supplies and accidentally stepped on a tube of paint. I tried to help her, but she wouldn't let me." She clasped her hands and looked at the teacher angelically. But she was far from the angel she pretended to be.

"That's not true!" Katherine cried. She begged her daughter to tell her teacher the truth. I crossed my fingers, but to my dismay Gabbie didn't utter a discriminating word.

It was Mrs. Jones who helped Gabbie to her feet. "You need to go to the nurse," the teacher said. "She can help you wash the paint off your face. Melissa will take you there."

Melissa's bony fingers found their way around Gabbie's wrist. As soon as the teacher returned to the classroom, the helping hand tightened.

"If you ever say anything about this, I'll hurt you," Melissa sneered. "I mean it. You'll wish you were never born." She gritted her teeth, twisting Gabbie's wrist tighter. "*Got it?*"

Chapter Fourteen
Mrs. Lavish

The nurse's office was on the second floor. When Gabbie arrived, she was glad to see it deserted. She couldn't deal with any other students laughing at her.

"My, my," said the jolly nurse as the girls entered the office. "What happened here?"

Melissa elbowed Gabbie in the side. "She fell. When she tried to get up, her hand pushed down on one of the tubes of paint. It squirted all over her. I rushed her here as fast as I could," she explained.

I had never heard Melissa's voice so soft, or so full of concern, or so full of doodly dung. Maybe she should take up drama. With a performance like this one, I'm sure she could win an Academy Award.

Gabbie rolled her lips in keeping Melissa's secret.

The nurse took Gabbie's hand. "You poor child." She led her to the washroom. "Come, let's wash that paint off your face."

Melissa followed dutifully behind them. If I hadn't known that she was the one who caused all this chaos, I would've bought what she was selling—hook, line, and sinker. Or was it *hook, lie,* and *stinker?*

"What is your name, dear?" Nurse Lavish asked.

Gabbie sniffed. She was so upset she hardly remembered her name. "Ga...briella Flowers."

"Gabriella Flowers? Aren't you the young lady who won the mural contest?"

Melissa's face squished up, just like it did when someone sucked on a lemon. Gabbie nodded her head reluctantly.

"Congratulations, that's quite exciting," Nurse Lavish said.

A small dark-skinned woman magically appeared and tapped Nurse Lavish on her shoulder. Her hair was long and black and reached clear down to her ankles. In the middle of her forehead was a red dot. Exactly where the third eye would be. Her name was Goulda. She was Nurse Lavish's guide and she just informed her that something wasn't quite right.

Mrs. Lavish looked at Gabbie. Then she looked at Melissa. Sensing something peculiar, she sent Melissa on her way.

But Melissa wasn't letting her grip go that easily. "No, I'll stay and wait for my friend." Melissa squeezed Gabbie's hand hard, as if to say, *remember what I told you.*

But the nurse insisted she leave. And when she did, Gabbie finally exhaled.

"Would you like me to call you mother?" The nurse asked.

Tell the nurse everything. You're safe, I promise, I said to Gabbie. But just like before, Gabbie's fear stopped her from speaking up.

"I live with my Nana. And I don't want you to call her. It's no big deal. She knows I'm a really clumsy. I'll just tell her when I get home. I promise."

After the nurse washed the paint from Gabbie's face, rinsed it from her eyes, and wiped it from her hair, the nurse let her rest until the end of the morning lesson. I sat on the edge of the cot trying to think of a way to help her. Katherine joined us.

"How is she?"

I let out a breath. "Not good," I said.

"Why isn't she asking for help?"

I sighed and shook my head. *Her fear is too strong. I'm afraid she's losing faith.*

Katherine's eyes grew wide with worry. She knew that if Gabbie's fear caused her to lose faith, then I'd disappear from her consciousness. And if I disappeared from her consciousness, then Gabbie wouldn't remember astral traveling, and if she didn't remember astral traveling she wouldn't remember visiting with her mother.

"Isn't there anything we can do?" Katherine asked.

"I'm afraid there isn't. We just have to wait," I answered.

"For how long" she asked.

I heard the panic in her voice. "If I could tell you I would, but there are so many variables. Let's just hope for all our sakes that she asks for help soon." Because if she doesn't everything she holds dear is doomed.

Katherine dropped a penny down on the pillow, right next to Gabbie's head. Gabbie rolled over and faced the wall. Either she didn't see it, or she no longer cared. Katherine looked at me. "What do we now?" She asked chewing on her lip.

The truth was, I had no idea. But I was determined to find out.

When lunchtime came, Gabbie reluctantly left the safety of the nurse's office. She carried the box of painting supplies to the ugly green wall designated for this year's mural. She put the box down and sat down next to it. She thought about eating her lunch, but she had no appetite, which was just as well. It was egg salad day.

"I don't even know where to start," she sighed. The thrill of winning the mural contest vanished like the white paint the nurse had washed off her skin. If only she hadn't called on the masters. She kicked the box in frustration. *I wish I never won this stupid contest.* But she did, and she knew she had to paint it. So she scooted to the box and took out a pencil. As soon as she started to draw, the pains in her belly went away and her joy found its way back into her heart. I checked my extremities to see if maybe, just maybe, I too, might be back, but just like before I was a mere memory of my former self.

Time passed faster than it had all week. The warning bell rang before Gabbie knew it. She had five minutes to pack up her supplies. She stood back to get a look at her progress. Two dragonflies graced the wall. Tomorrow she would pencil in the words.

Tubes of paint flew through the air, some landing in the box, and others bouncing off the sides. Gabbie wanted to get to the classroom before the bell rang. She didn't want to risk bumping into Melissa. There was no telling what she would do now that the mural was in full swing.

Before she could gather the last of her supplies, the bell rang. The corridor was quickly packed with students. "Drats," Gabbie said. She picked up the box and looked over her shoulder. Melissa was hard to miss; between her obnoxious cackle and her giant stature, she stood heads above her classmates. Gabbie ducked into a doorway and pressed her body tight against the wall hoping to go unnoticed.

It worked.

Melissa and Camille stopped and looked up at the mural.

"I can't believe that stupid painting won. It must've been fixed. There is no way this was better than mine!" Melissa snickered.

Camille shrugged. "I like it," she said.

Gabbie peeked out from the doorway just in time to see Melissa's reaction. Melissa pushed Camille so hard that she stumbled to the ground and bounced a few times before coming to a stop. Gabbie gasped. She wanted to do something. She wanted to help. But her body was frozen with fear.

Chapter Fifteen
Fight... Fight... Fight...

abbie chewed on her bottom lip. *Hurry up, hurry up*, she thought as she waited on the curb. All she wanted to do was get this day over with.

The cars aren't moving too quickly, she thought. *Maybe I could dart through them.* She was quick. And small. And if she thought she could have gotten away with it, she might have taken the risk. But she knew she couldn't. If something happened to her, what would it do to her Nana's heart?

Gabbie couldn't think of a more magnificent sound than the sound of the crossing guard's whistle. It blared through the air, piercing her eardrums. But to Gabbie it was the sound of angels coming to her rescue.

Two blocks later, I told Gabbie to run. I don't know if she heard me, or the sound of feet pounding on the sidewalk. Whatever it was, it got her attention. She took off running. I've never seen her run so fast. She scooted between a man with a tiny dog on a leash and a woman pushing a double baby stroller. She almost collided with an elderly woman pulling a grocery cart. The old woman shook her head and mumbled under her breath.

"Sorry!" Gabbie shouted, though it didn't slow her pace. It couldn't. Melissa was gaining ground. Her legs were so much longer than Gabbie's; for every two steps of Gabbie's, Melissa only had to take one.

A flush of nervous energy raced through my soul. I wish I could've picked her up and flown her home. Wouldn't that be something? I could only imagine the look on Melissa's face when she witnessed Gabbie flying.

Dean was racing alongside Melissa, shouting through his megaphone. Mildred tended to Camille, who was sitting in the middle of the sidewalk panting for breath. Gabbie dropped her backpack hoping to gain some speed. *Great idea*, I told her. Melissa had to swerve to the left in order to avoid it. She twirled and swung her arms around in circles, but she didn't fall. "I'll get you for that!" she hollered.

Gabbie didn't look back. She raced around the corner, breathing heavily as she ran. Though she did the best she could, it wasn't long before Melissa caught up. She reached out and grabbed Gabbie's collar with her long skinny fingers.

"Urgh!" Gabbie grunted as Melissa stopped her forward motion. Gabbie's chest bowed out and her feet flew out from beneath her. A pair of metal garbage cans sat on the sidewalk. It was a disaster in the making.

Gabbie fell backward, smacking into Melissa. Melissa fell backward into the garbage cans. It was hard to watch.

Arms and legs were everywhere. They looked like alley cats fighting over a scrap of food.

I was so glad Katherine had gone back to heaven. I would have hated for her to witness this. A few kids from school gathered around the pair rolling in the garbage cans. A woman walking on the other side of the street glanced their way, but she was too busy talking on her cell phone to really take notice. Camille ran up to the scene, red in the face and breathing hard. In her hand was her inhaler. She tried to see what was happening, but the circle of kids blocked her view. She rose up on her tippy toes, but it didn't help, so she bent down and looked between their legs.

I paced the sidewalk unsure of what to do. *The Spirit Guide Handbook* was clear and I knew I couldn't intervene, but I had to do something, fast. *Please God, you gotta help my girl*, I prayed. Just then, a flash of light appeared. With it came a thunderous rumble, catching everyone's attention.

It was a motorcycle.

It came roaring to a stop right where the girls were fighting.

A man with a silver beard wearing a green motorcycle jacket sat on the gleaming green Harley. A pair of dark goggles covered his eyes. Next to him, tucked in a sidecar, sat a woman dressed in a bright blue leather jacket.

"Hey, what's going on there?" the man hollered.

Melissa, along with the group of students who had gathered to watch, took off running. I breathed out a sigh of relief. Though I was happy to see the odd looking couple, I wished it hadn't come to this.

"Are you all right, dear?" the woman asked Gabbie. Her voice was calm and soothing. She climbed off the motorcycle and reached down to give Gabbie a hand. Her touch sent goose bumps to Gabbie's skin and a peaceful feeling to her soul.

"Yes, I think so," Gabbie said. After she straightened her blouse and smoothed down her skirt, she looked up to thank the woman, but the motorcycle and the couple were gone.

"Where did they go?" Gabbie said to Camille, who had sat on the curb to take a whiff out of her inhaler.

"Who?" She managed to say in between huffs.

Chapter Sixteen
Another Lie

Gabbie climbed the stoop of the old brownstone. She closed the door slowly and covered the latch with her hand, hoping to absorb the sound of the click. She tiptoed over the wooden floor. She thought if she could make it upstairs before Nana spotted her, she had a chance of keeping the fight to herself.

She placed her right foot on the first step and slowly pressed down. The first step was a major squeaker. She winced every time a step threatened to give her away. By the time she made it to the top of the staircase, she was blue and out of breath.

She knew if Nana saw the spots of paint splattered across her uniform, she'd have to explain, so she rolled up her shirt and skirt and shoved them behind her dresser. She tiptoed into the bathroom and gritted her teeth as she turned on the water. The old copper pipes gurgled and moaned. "Pleeeeaaassseee... be quiet," she whispered. Scrapes covered her elbows and knees. After she washed the blood from her skin, she moved her fingers gently over her scalp. She winced when she found what she was looking for. The bump was the size of a robin's egg and very tender to the touch. It had hatched moments after she collided with Melissa on the street. The bruise on her wrist had turned a deep purple. And Gabbie knew from past experiences that a bruise that dark took at least two weeks to fade away. She would have to come up with some convincing tale on how it got there, knowing it would be hard to cover her arms for that long a time. After all, it was spring now and the air was lovely and warm.

Though for today, until she thought of something foolproof, she would have to find something to cover her arms. She searched her bottom drawer for the perfect disguise.

Nana Alice was in the back courtyard watering the flowers. Gabbie pushed through the back door. It banged behind her.

"Hi, Nana. How was your day?" she asked beneath a bulky sweatshirt and a pair of thick jeans. Her arms hugged each other at the elbows and there was a fake smile draped across her face.

"Are you cold?" Nana asked. There had to be a reason why her granddaughter was dressed so warmly. She put down the watering can and placed her hand on Gabbie's forehead. "Maybe you're coming down with something."

Gabbie tugged at the sleeve of her sweatshirt. "I'm fine," she said. She wrapped her arms tighter around her waist while holding the edges of her sleeves. Nana placed her hands on the sides of Gabbie's face. "I'm okay, really, I am," Gabbie said through her squished up lips.

Nana bent down. "Is that paint in your hair?"

Tell her Gabbie, now's your chance.

Nana started to push the hair off Gabbie's face, but before she could run her hand over her head, Gabbie backed away.

Where was Dean with his giant megaphone when you needed him? I thought. Magically, a megaphone suddenly appeared in my hand. I snorted. *It's worth a try.*

I placed the megaphone next to Gabbie's ear. *Now! Tell her, now! This is your chance!* I shouted. *Tell her what's been happening.*

Gabbie flinched.

Hooray!

But a second later, my enthusiasm rushed out of my soul like a balloon losing air. Gabbie didn't tell her Nana what I told her to say. Instead she said it was nothing. "Just a little paint. I started the mural today."

Urgggghhhhhh!!!!!!! I wrapped my fingers around my hair. If I pull any harder I'll end up looking like a stray cat with mange. I knew Gabbie was stubborn but this is ridiculous.

What else can I do? If I could I'd pick something up I'd throw it as hard as I could. All this pent up frustration is driving me insane.

Later that night, I sat on the edge of Gabbie's bed. She was rolled up tight in a ball. She couldn't stop the tears from streaming down her face. She tried to sob into her pillow, but it made it hard to breathe.

Victoria got out of bed. She sat next to me as I sat next to her sister. "Are you okay?" she asked Gabbie, placing her hand gently on her shoulder.

Tell her what happened today, Gabbie, I said. I was sure she wouldn't tell her sister what's been going on but to my surprise she did. She told her about the kicking, the flying rubber bands, and the squirting paint. She even showed her the bruise still wrapped around her wrist. She was so close to asking for help I could almost taste it.

"Do you want me to get Nana?" Victoria asked.

Yes, that's a great idea, I said. But Gabbie said no. *If skinning her chin could be the death of her Nana how would she handle this?* She wondered. Her cries became steadier. Her upper lip swelled, and her nose began to run.

"If you don't want to tell Nana what's going on, I could call Daddy," Victoria said.

Yes, that's a wonderful idea. Call Michael, I said.

That—along with all the other good ideas—vanished when Gabbie shook her head. *If you called him, he'd tell Nana what's been going on,* she thought. So no, she didn't want her sister to call him.

Madeline made a suggestion.

"What a fabulous idea," I said. I picked her up and swung her around. If I couldn't get through to Gabbie, maybe Madeline could use her sister.

Madeline's request drifted into Victoria's head and popped into her mind as a brilliant idea. "I know," Victoria said. "Why don't you pray to God for help?"

This is it, I thought. I clasped my hands together waiting for Gabbie to ask for help. But to my dismay she didn't.

Instead, she shook her head and sniffled. "I can't. He's mad at me," she said.

My brows knitted together. *What? That's not true!* I told Madeline to tell Victoria that God *wasn't* mad at her, and Victoria repeated it to Gabbie.

"Then why is he doing this to me?" she asked.

Victoria sighed. "I don't know."

I thought this would be the night when Gabbie finally asked for help. But it wasn't. She just cried until she fell asleep.

Chapter Seventeen
Blood...Blood...Everywhere

The following morning, Gabbie tried to stay home from school, but to her dismay she did not have a fever, she did not have the flu, she did not have the mumps or chicken pox. She did not have a rash, nothing was broken and no, she did not have gas, which, by the way, is the cause of most bellyaches, Nana had once said. So off to school she went.

As she walked to school, I watched Nana pick up the telephone. Two Feather's said he sent Nana a feeling. It stirred in her stomach. Something was not right with her youngest granddaughter and she was determined to get to the bottom of it.

I crossed my fingers. This might be the break I was hoping for.

After speaking with Mrs. Jones on the phone, Nana was more confused than before. "Could it be I was wrong?" she said.

Mrs. Jones had said nothing strange was happening. As far as she knew, anyway. "But I'll be sure to call you if I see anything," the teacher had said.

I threw my hands up in frustration. *How many people is it going to take to put an end to this,* I wondered.

The morning showed no sign of improving as the green-eyed monster sat directly behind Gabbie. Gabbie endured it all with little hope of it going away. The latest attempt of bullying failed only because Gabbie bent down to scratch a sudden itch on her shin.

To my delight, Katherine had showed up just in the nick of time. She had dragged her finger along Gabbie's skin. Thankfully, Gabbie narrowly avoided the heavy book that crashed against the back of her chair instead of her head.

"What are you doing here?" I asked. "Not that I'm *not* grateful for you interference, I am, but I thought I told you to stay back *there*." I shook my head. "I mean back *here*."

"I couldn't stay *there*. I mean *here*. Not while she's... *here*," Katherine said.

It was the flying desk that finally grabbed Mrs. Jones's attention.

Melissa had used her foot to kick Gabbie's desk halfway across the room. It flew into another desk, tilted over, and landed with a bang on its side. Gabbie tried her older sister's advice, but it was hard to ignore the contents of her desk littering the floor.

"What on earth are you doing, Miss Flowers?"

She looked at the teacher, her eyes were as large as a deer's staring into a pair of headlights. Melissa stood with her hands on her stomach, giggling under her breath. Her shoulders shook uncontrollably.

"Tell her the truth!" Katherine shouted.

She rushed towards Mrs. Jones. "Please, Mrs. Jones, please help my daughter." But the teacher didn't hear her. All the teacher heard was bouts of laughter coming from the girl who was bullying Katherine's daughter.

Katherine began to sob. *"Please, someone help my daughter!"*

It was Camille who answered her plea. She pointed toward Melissa behind the shield of her hand. Unfortunately, the teacher didn't notice, but Melissa did.

Melissa's lip trembled as she glared at Camille. Camille gasped.

Don't do it. Don't do it, Dean warned.

Of course, Melissa didn't listen. And when the teacher wasn't looking, Melissa pushed Camille as hard as she could.

Mildred squeezed her eyes shut. She couldn't bare to witness it.

Katherine shouted, *"No!"*

But the damage was done.

Camille went flying forward. "Whoa!"

Gabbie reached out to help her, but Camille stumbled to the ground.

"Oomph!" Camille grunted.

"Are you okay?" Gabbie asked. When she reached down to help her friend stand up, Gabbie noticed blood running from Camille's nose.

It wasn't uncommon for Camille's nose to start bleeding for no good reason, and as soon as Melissa saw the blood drip on to Camille's blouse, she used it to her advantage.

"Ewh!" Melissa shouted. Her long lanky finger pointed at Gabbie. "She hit her! Did you see that? Gabbie hit Camille in the nose!"

While Camille was tending to her nosebleed in the nurse's office, Gabbie sat in the principal's office. Thankfully, Katherine went back to Heaven. I told her it wouldn't do her or her daughter any good if she lost her temper.

By now there was nothing left of me but that spirit guide glow. I was totally invisible. Even to Gabbie. I searched her mind for any mention of my name, and there was none. If she were still able to hear my voice, it would be so high that it would come across as a mere ringing in her ear. If I didn't think of some way to get through to her—and I mean right then—I was sure to be a goner.

The clock ticked loudly as each second passed. Gabbie's eyes glazed over. I concentrated on her thoughts. I needed to know what was going through her mind. There was one thought that kept rolling around in her mind. Saint

Anne's. It rolled around over and over just like the second hand of the clock. Her belly twisted, and she felt sick to her stomach. Her head fell heavily into her hands.

Saint Anne's? Why does that ring a bell?

It took a second, but it came back to me. For a month, after Mr. Fiddlydinks jumped from the stoop and broke Mr. Warsinski's favorite pot, Gabbie had dreamed about Saint Anne's, and by the look on her face she was back in the same nightmare as she sat waiting to learn her fate. Her skin was pure white and her hands trembled. I stilled my mind so I could read hers. I was right; her imagination had whisked her away to a place she never wanted to go.

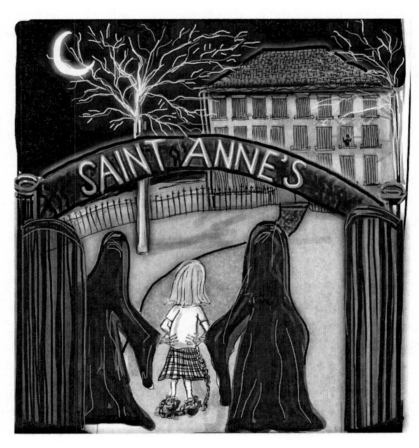

Dried dead leaves crunched beneath Gabbie's feet as she dragged the heavy metal shackles along the path to her doom. It lead to an an old brick building with barred windows. The sign above the entrance read: Saint Anne's Reform School. Gloom filled Gabbie's mind as the wind whistled through the bare trees. It was as if the trees were mocking her, laughing at her misfortune, telling her she got what she deserved.

"I didn't do it. I'm innocent, innocent, innocent." Her words echoed through the barren woods. "I'm innocent, innocent, *innocent!*"

The huge front door opened on its own. The metal scrapped across the floor. *Uuurrr!* It made Gabbie's skin ripple with goose bumps. Her hair stood at attention. She was never so scarred in her life. A pair of hooded figures appeared at her side. They wore thick black cloaks concealing their identities. A hand, consisting of only bones, seized her by the wrist. It squeezed her arm so tightly Gabbie screamed out in pain.

"Ouch!" she cried. She didn't want to; she just couldn't help it.

The cloaked figure turned and faced her. Instead of it being Mr. Warsinski like it had been in her nightmare, now it was a girl.

A very mean girl.

A girl with wired fangs.

The girl's stringy brown hair peeked out from the hood, and cheese hung from her braces. "Still crying, crybaby?" A piercing cry filled the air as Melissa let out the most evil cackle Gabbie had ever heard.

Gabbie clapped her hands over her ears trying to make the laughter stop. The hood of the second figure slipped, revealing another girl who looked exactly like Melissa. In fact, everyone in the great hall looked just like Melissa. The girl's shoulders shook from the burst of giggles beneath the cloak, but Gabbie couldn't tell if it was really Melissa or one of her clones.

Another Melissa sat high behind a desk with a plaque, which read *Warden*. She grinned at Gabbie wickedly. Her teeth were pointy and made of steel. Instead of stringy brown hair that lay flat on her head, this Melissa had hair that stretched off her face forming two horns, which glowed bright red.

"Well, well, well, if it isn't the crybaby! Lock her in the dungeon," the warden growled.

"No, please no!" Gabbie cried.

A hideous laugh filled the air. All the clones crept toward her. Gabbie tried to run, but the chains were way too heavy.

Chapter Eighteen
Sentencing

"Miss Flowers?"

It was the third time Mrs. Hannel had called Gabbie's name.

"Huh?" Gabbie said, shaking her day-mare from her head. She looked at the secretary with glazed over eyes.

The secretary repeated herself. "Mr. Ward will see you now." The secretary went back to painting her nails. A glob of red lacquer dripped off the brush and fell to the floor, pooling on the tile like blood. Gabbie stared at the nail polish. Panic surged through her veins.

The door to the principal's office opened slowly. Mr. Ward stepped out and peered over his spectacles. He stood over six feet tall, filling the doorway completely.

Gabbie's mind was racing. The principal was even bigger than the warden in her nightmare. *Oh, please God ...*

I jumped to my feet. This is it. She's finally going to ask for help. *Say it, say it. Please Gabbie ask for help!*

Her heart bounced against her chest like a basketball, and yet she still didn't ask for help. All she was thinking was *Please God, don't let them send me to Saint Anne's.*

My arms dropped to my sides. All my hope drained from my fingers into a puddle on the floor.

The principal's office was nothing like she had imagined. There weren't any chains or torturing devices. There wasn't a guillotine, or any scary creatures cloaked in black. It was just your average office. There were two chairs in front of a desk, bookshelves, and some filing cabinets.

Gabbie took a seat. Her heart was racing. She wrung her hands together. I hovered above her, too nervous to sit. The only thing I had to hope for now was that her fear of Saint Anne's was greater than her fear of the bully in the classroom.

The principal's phone rang. "Excuse me for a moment," he said politely. Gabbie watched Mr. Ward scribble on his notepad. He nodded. "Yes, I see."

You see what? Gabbie wondered. She tried to make out who the caller was but couldn't. All she heard was a female voice mumbling away. She rubbed her belly and tried to swallow. Her mind was going wild. She just twisted her fingers together until Mr. Ward said, "Yes. Thank you," and hung the phone back on the receiver.

After adjusting his glasses, Principal Ward placed his pen down. He laced his fingers, and rocked back in his chair. A knot jammed in Gabbie's throat, making it hard for her breathe.

"That was Nurse Lavish on the phone," the principal finally said. "And after hearing Camille Wilson's account of the event, it seems Miss Graves has a lot to learn about losing gracefully."

"Really?" Gabbie gasped. She was sure the news on the phone hadn't been good. "Does the mean you're not going to send me to Saint Anne's?"

"Oh, goodness, no," the principal chuckled. "You're not being sent to Saint Anne's. I'm sorry this happened to you. No one should have to fear a bully. And I can assure you, we will put an end to it."

Goose bumps raced up and down Gabbie's arms. She couldn't believe her luck. Her troubles were over. And she didn't have to give anything up.

I, on the other hand, wasn't so enthused. According to Gabbie's chart, since she didn't ask for help, this mess would continue for the rest of the school year, which meant Gabbie would be bullied for another month.

Principal Ward smiled at her and closed the folder. From the folder came a shiny copper coin. The penny rolled off the desk and landed on Gabbie's lap.

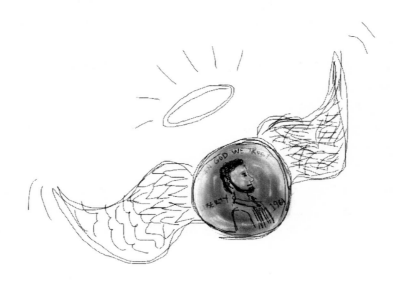

"Humm ... where did that come from?" he asked.

Gabbie smiled. "It's from my mom. She sent it from heaven."

Chapter Nineteen
Run!

Gabbie skipped along the sidewalk thinking the bullying was finally over. Mr. Ward transferred Melissa to Mr. Butler's class, and she had nothing to do with it.

I stood at the curb with Gabbie as she waited to cross the street, alone.

Miss Turner blew the whistle and marched bravely into the oncoming traffic. Her white gloved hand was head high over her red spikey hair. The piercing shrill of her whistle rang through the air. The speeding cars came to a screeching halt. Once we had crossed, Ms. Turner blew her whistle and cars continued on their way.

I continued to watch the school building for Melissa. Dean had warned me, she was piping mad. Even madder than she had been when Gabbie stole the mural contest from her. She was going to make Gabbie pay. No one tattles on Melissa Graves and gets away with it.

She raced from the school building, dragging Camille by her backpack. "Drats!" she shouted. They were too late. She paced the sidewalk. With each step she took her face grew redder. "This is your fault you dweeb. If you didn't have to go back to your locker for that stupid inhaler, we could've caught her."

Mildred gave Dean a high five. *A forgotten inhaler just bought my girl, and me, a little more time.*

"I'm sorry," Camille said quietly. But she really wasn't.

Melissa took a hold of her arm and marched her away from Ms. Turner. If they were to catch up with Gabbie they'd have to cross to avenue now.

"I don't want to cross here," Camille cried when they reached the busy intersection.

Melissa ignored her. With a hand on the strap of Camille's backpack they weaved through the oncoming traffic. A truck screeched to a halt. The driver's hand shook out the window, violently. "I could have killed you, you stupid kids."

Melissa marched on, unaffected. Camille however, struggled to breathe. She stopped to fish her inhaler out of her backpack getting more anxious with each labored breath.

"I don't have time to waste on your stupid inhaler," Melissa barked and took off running.

"No, stop!" Camille shouted, but it was hardly a whisper. Mildred had told me she had told Camille to stand up to Melissa, too, but to her dismay Camille's fear was just as strong as Gabbie's.

Melissa's skinny legs picked up the pace. Her arms swung crazy at her side.

Run home as fast as you can, I said pointing behind us. I wasn't sure if Gabbie could hear me, but thankfully she turned to look. When Gabbie saw Melissa running toward us, she threw her backpack over her shoulder and begun to run as fast as she could.

Keep running and don't stop, I told her. For the first time in a month, Gabbie did exactly as I told her.

The number one rule of guiding a soul while on earth is: Never interfere. Ever. No matter the reason. And if I were to do so, well, I could be fired. And that would be a first.

Surely a garage can or two rolled precisely in Melissa's path couldn't be considered interfering, could it? I really wasn't sure, but I was willing to take the risk.

I squeezed between a few metal garbage cans. If I just pushed one out, just a bit, it might throw off her pace, leaving enough time for Gabbie to get home unharmed.

I wrapped my arms around the can and used every ounce of energy I had. "Urgh!" It didn't move, not even a hair. I pounded my fist against it. If I were going to move this thing a few feet, I needed to figure out another way—and quickly.

Think, think, think. I pulled my hands through my hair. What else could I do? I'd asked her countless times to ask for help. I couldn't intervene; only angels could do that. Then a burst of hope popped into my head. *I'm the one who could ask for help!* Why didn't I think of that before? So I sent up a prayer, just like I wanted Gabbie to do. *Okay God, I need a little divine intervention here.*

The words no sooner left my lips than a door to my left opened. "Get out, get out," an elderly woman said. "Go back to where you came from." The black cat hissed and raised a white paw.

Is that? Can it be? Mr. Fiddlydinks?

Mr. Fiddlydinks hopped onto the railing between the stoops. He looked directly at me, totally aware of my presence.

That's it! I thought. If I couldn't move the can, maybe I could get something to move it for me. I waited on the stoop for the precise moment to jump into action. The timing had to be perfect. If it wasn't, I risked more than I cared to think about. Melissa stomped down the sidewalk, her arms waving at her sides. "You better run fast, you snitching crybaby!"

Ready ...

Melissa ran closer.

I crouched down close to Mr. Fiddlydinks' ear. It twitched.

Get set ...

One more step. I took a deep breath.

Go!

"*Aaaaarrrggghhh!*" I shouted, as loud as I could, straight into the cat's ear.

And just as planned, Mr. Fiddlydinks freaked out. He jumped off the porch like a rocket and soared through the air, paws out. "*Meow!*" he screeched when he landed on the sidewalk.

It worked. Mr. Fiddlydinks got tangled in Melissa's limbs. "Get off me you stupid beast!" With a kick and a yank, Melissa freed herself, but it didn't matter. Enough time was gained and Gabbie was safe inside her house. At least for another day.

Chapter Twenty
The Elders

abbie climbed the stairs to her room. With each lumbered step she thought about Melissa. *How am I ever going to get through this?* She wondered. She took a seat on the stairs. She sighed, heavily, and rested her head in her hands. "Samuel, where are you?" Tears welled in her eyes.

I'm right here, I said waving my hands in front of her face. But her eyes looked right through me.

Maybe Victoria was right, she thought. *Maybe Samuel was just a figment of my imagination. Maybe all of it was just a silly old dream.* Tears streamed down her face. *Maybe I wanted to be with Mama so badly I made it all up.*

Then I experienced an emotion I hadn't experienced since the last time I was in earth school. Anger rose through my body and exploded in my head. There was no way I was going to let Gabbie go!

I whipped *The Spirit Guide Handbook* open, though I had no idea what I was looking for. Skimming over the table of contents I found a section called: When All Else Fails. This situation (*I believed*) fell perfectly into that category. Now all I had to do was hope the Elders thought so too.

A moment later, as I sat with Gabbie on the stairs, I bi-located to heaven. I wasn't there, or *here* but a moment when Katherine appeared by my side. "So how did it go?" she asked as we raced up the stone steps of the *Hall of Justice*. It looked just like the other main temples in heaven built in the Romanesque theme. Large columns graced the entrance and a golden dome sat on top.

"Well, Melissa was removed from Gabbie's class," I said as we entered the hall.

"That's great!" she shouted.

"Yup," I replied. It was all I could manage. I was too busy worrying about a plan for small talk.

Katherine frowned. "Is there a problem?"

I nodded my head. "She still hasn't asked for help."

"What? I thought you said Melissa was removed from her class."

"I did, but still hasn't asked for help. She's lost faith."

"Oh Samuel, we can't fade away. There must be something you can do?" she said as she struggled to keep up with me. "I'm not going to lose my baby, not again."

"I called an emergency meeting with the Elder's. Maybe they can help."

We wound our way through the halls until we found the *Council of Elders.* Also known as the Master Teachers, the Elders are a group of twenty-two highly evolved entities who help souls who have incarnated to earth, and their guides too.

Though all souls *here* looked to be about thirty years old, (Why? I have no idea, they just do), the Elders all sport long white or graying hair. The males had long beards that touched the gold medallion they all wore over their flowing lavender robes.

The council members sat behind a U-shaped table with the hierarchy sitting in the middle. The Elder named Malachi motioned towards us. Katherine and I approached the bench.

"Thank you for seeing us," I said nervously. If I couldn't convince them to help us, Katherine and I would have no other choice than to watch Gabbie go through life without our help. And neither one of us could bare to see that happen.

"It is our pleasure," Malachi said. "How may we be of assistance?"

Katherine stood next to me fiddling with the key hanging around her neck. Still unsure of how to proceed, I thought I might as well just tell the Elders why we came before them. With their infinite knowledge, maybe they could offer a solution. So I took a breath and began.

"As you know, Gabriella is riddled with fear. She hasn't asked for help and she's questioning my existence. I know we cannot change the lessons in which she has to learn. But I was hoping... maybe...uhm..."

Katherine interrupted me. I was glad because I didn't have a clue what we could do. I thought (no, make that hoped) that some miraculous idea would've popped into my head. But it seemed any idea missed my mind and went into hers instead.

"We could give Gabbie something to remind her that this plane *does* exist. We're real and if she asks for help, she will receive it."

The Elders sat silently but I knew they were conversing telepathically. I couldn't hear them discuss Katherine's plea and yet I knew they were taking the utmost care in its consideration. Her idea *was* fabulous and it wouldn't interfere with Gabbie's plan or the lessons she went to earth to learn. When the council arrived at a conclusion they smiled at us in unison.

Malachi stood. "We have come to a decision," he said. One of Katherine's hands gripped mine and the other fiddled with the key. "When and if Gabriella asks for help, you *may* give her a token to help remind her of all the power she possesses."

"Oh, thank you, thank you so much," Katherine said. She turned and hugged me.

"Oh Samuel. Just one more thing."

I turned to look at the head Elder. My heart rose to my throat. *Was he going to reprimand me for interfering in Gabbie's plan?*

"Very inventive way to use a cat."

"Thank you, Sir," I said relieved.

Malachi took his seat. I bowed and thanked them, then Katherine and I headed out of the room.

Twirling around in the middle of the corridor Katherine could not hold back her enthusiasm. She sang as she twirled. "Isn't this wonderful?"

"There's only one problem," I said.

Katherine stopped mid-spin. "And what would that be?"

"Gabbie still hasn't asked for help. And if she doesn't, she won't be astral traveling anytime soon."

Katherine frowned. "Can't you pull her soul out of her body the next time she falls asleep?" she asked.

"It's against the rules. Besides, I don't think it's possible," I said. But I wasn't about to give up on Gabbie just yet. If I had to move heaven and earth, I was going to find a way.

My eyes grew wide as an idea entered my head. If I couldn't move things, I knew just the soul who could.

I grabbed Katherine's hand. "Come on, let's go."

Chapter Twenty - One
Finally

As I sat with Gabbie on the staircase I bi-located to her bedroom with Katherine. I dragged her to the dresser and pointed to the jar where Gabbie kept the pennies she had sent her. My heart was beating so fast I could hardly breathe. "I need you to write her a message with the pennies," I said.

Katherine clapped her hands together. "What a wonderful idea." She shook the pennies out of the jar. Then she arranged them one by one on Gabbie's bed. It was a good thing the spread was white. The raised pile of the chenille made the coins tilt in different directions, yet Katherine was able to position the pennies into a legible word.

Just as she placed the last coin into position, Gabbie walked into the room. Her face was as long as a late afternoon shadow. One part of me stood next to the bed while another part walked into the room. Gabbie sighed and threw her backpack listlessly toward the chair next to the dresser. Katherine raced toward the chair. Right before the bag came to a rest on the cushion, she kicked a leg, causing the bag to fall to the floor with a bang. Out of the backpack rolled a penny.

"You're a genius," I said as my soul merged back together. I forgot about the penny she had sent Gabbie while she was in the principal's office. A smile stretched across Katherine's face. And then one stretched across her daughter's. "Could it be?" Gabbie said. The penny rolled under the dresser. There was barely enough room for her hand. She wrinkled her nose as she wiggled her fingers. The dust, rolled up like bunnies, scurried across the floor making her sneeze. She bounced her hand under the dresser until her fingers hit something cold. Something round. She pinched the penny between her fingers and gently drew it out. When she went to place the coin in the jar, she noticed it was gone. She swung around with her hands clenched at her sides, determined to blame her sister for its disappearance.

"Victoria! Did you … ?" She started to yell at her sister even though she was not in the room. She stopped mid-sentence. A ray of sunshine streamed through the window. It stretched across the room and ended at the pennies spread across the bed. The coins twinkled like diamonds and spelled out the word *pray.* Gabbie's eyes grew wide.

"Whoo-hoo!" I hollered. I wrapped Katherine in my arms and spun her around. I couldn't believe it. It worked! Soon Gabbie would be down on her knees asking for the help she so desperately needed.

But my celebration was cut short as her thoughts echoed through my mind, stopping my twirling of Katherine mid-spin. *Why would Mama tell me to pray?*

Sensing my fear, Katherine placed her hand on my shoulder. "She's a smart girl; she'll figure it out."

I hope she's right, for all our sakes.

Gabbie sighed as she sat gently on the bed so as not to disturb her mother's message. *Could asking God for help really solve my problem?* She wondered.

Yes! I screamed. *It's that's simple.*

Gabbie slid to her knees beside the bed and laced her fingers together. She bowed her head. *"Please God, if you can still hear me, I need your help."*

My hands flew in the air. "Hallelujah!" I exclaimed.

"We did it!" Katherine said, jumping with excitement.

Suddenly, Gabbie was overcome by exhaustion, all the fear, and worry had taken its toll. She climbed on the bed careful not to disturb her mother's message. As soon as she laid her head down on the pillow she fell fast asleep. And when she did, her soul lifted out of her body. "Where have you been?" She asked me, angrily.

My spirit became solid once again. Relieved I said, "I've been here all along. But I faded from your consciousness because you built a wall of fear between us."

She lowered her eyes. "I'm sorry," she said. "But the bullying was *so* frightening."

"You're right, it can be, but that is when you need me the most."

I held out my hand. "There's something I've been wanting to show you, something that can stop the bullying, once and for all. So are you ready?"

Gabbie nodded. "I'm more than ready."

She took my hand and flew towards heaven.

We soared over a field of bright red poppies, reminding Gabbie of the scene in the *Wizard of Oz*. But instead of the Emerald City, the *Temple of Reconnection* stood at the edge of the poppy field.

When we touched down on the steps of the temple, Katherine rushed towards her daughter, arms wide. Gabbie ran into her mother's open arms. "I'm so happy to see you, love," her mother said.

It was a joyful reunion, one that—a few hours earlier—I hadn't been sure would ever happen again.

As Gabbie hugged her mother, a familiar sound hovered overhead. Her eyes grew wide. "Are those dragonflies?" she asked. She extended a finger hoping one of the dragonflies would land on it. The blue dragonfly granted her wish and placed its tiny feet upon her outstretched finger. Its wings came to a halt as it rested on its perch. Its eyes were bright and angelic. "Come follow us," it said. The dragonfly flew back into the air joining the green one. Gabbie grabbed her mother's hand and followed the pair down a cobblestone path.

Beyond the footbridges, behind a wall of cascading passion vine, the dragonflies hovered above a marble bench. Once seated, as if on cue, the dragonflies ascended high into the air and disappeared. Then, a cloud of stardust appeared and floated down to the ground. From the mist of twinkling light, the man dressed in green, and the woman in blue, emerged.

"Hey! You're the couple who saved me from Melissa," Gabbie shouted.

"May I present your Angels," Katherine said. "Tempest and Caroline."

Gabbie's jaw dropped.

"Not exactly the kind of Divine guidance you were expecting, right?" I said.

Gabbie thought of whispery angelic beings floating down from Heaven, not the couple that roared up on a Harley just in the knick of time to save her.

"I'm so sorry that happened to you, but I know of something that can help you," Caroline said. Her voice was soft and filled with unconditional love.

"How?" Gabbie asked.

"We're going to teach you how to defend yourself," I said.

"What, like kung fu?" Gabbie asked. She chopped her hands through the air. "I always wanted to learn kung fu."

"No," I laughed. "With *magic*."

Gabbie's eyes grew wide. "Magic? But how do *I* do that?"

"First you need to pick something that will help safeguard your energy." I said.

"Why? What's energy got to do with anything?"

"Everything," Katherine said. "Without the exchange of energy, Melissa won't be satisfied."

"Without energy she'll get bored and move on," I said.

"There are plenty of things you can use to ward off evil. You can surround yourself with mirrors and send the negative energy back to where it came from," Katherine suggested.

"Or a golden sword," I added. "There's gold and silver nets, or a dome of light."

Gabbie thought about it. She could not see herself surrounded by mirrors or wielding a sword through the air. She needed to come up with something, something magnificent. Moments passed as she thought about her options. Then, a simple conclusion literally popped into her mind. She raised her finger. "I got it! A bubble, like Gilda from the "Wizard of Oz," Gabbie said. She could easily imagine floating through the air as she glided over the evil in the playground.

"That's a wonderful idea," her mother said.

"Now all you have to do is summon your bubble and we will protect you," Tempest said. Caroline nodded her head in agreement."

Magically, a bubble surrounded Gabbie. Although it was clear, it had a rainbow film, just like one of those bubbles she blew from a wand—you know, the ones that come in a jar. But unlike one of those bubbles, this bubble couldn't be broken.

Gabbie poked her finger at the film expecting it to pop. It didn't. It just stretched out and then bounced back into place "This is *sooo* cool," she sang. "I wish I could float through the air."

No sooner did the words leave her lips than the bubble started to rise into the air.

One foot.
Two foot.
Three feet.
Four.
"I love heaven!" she sang. She rose so high she touched the pink sky.

Katherine encircled herself in the same fashion her daughter did and slowly she, too, began to rise from the ground. She spread her arms and legs to engulf the bubble as Gabbie did, cart wheeling through the air. As they both spun round and round their bubbles gently bumped each other pushing them in opposite directions. Gabbie laughed as if she never had before.

Chapter Twenty - Two
Bubble Bubble

As soon as her bubble touched the ground, the cord attached to Gabbie's belly started to glow. "Oh drats, just when it was getting good."

Katherine stooped down to look her daughter in the eye. She straightened Gabbie's shoulders and brushed down the sides of her hair. "I want you to have something." She reached inside her pocket and pulled out a golden key hanging from a red ribbon. "Here," Katherine said, dangling the key in front of Gabbie. "My parents gave me this when I was your age."

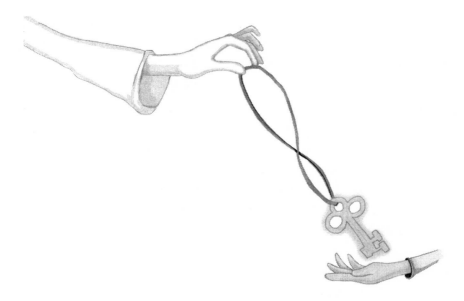

"What does it open?" Gabbie asked, unable to take her eyes off the key. It sparkled brighter than anything she'd ever seen.

"Everything," her mother said. She dropped the key into Gabbie's hand. "This key will remind you whenever you feel threatened, or lonely, or sad or mad, whenever you feel hopeless or scared, to call on God and your angels. It will remind you to call on your bubble. But most of all, it will remind you to send love to those who challenge you, for they are helping your soul grow."

Gabbie stuck her finger in her ear and wiggled it. "I could've sworn you just said you want me to send Melissa *love*."

"She did," I said as my arms rested across my chest. I knew Gabbie was going to have a problem with this part. Most humans do, and for the exact reason Gabbie was about to announce.

"She's terrorized me. She took away the best thing that ever happened to me and now you ..."

Without warning, the silver cord attached to Gabbie's stomach yanked her from where she stood. She flew through the pink sky, arms flailing. A second later her soul slammed into her body. "Whoa!" she shouted as she sprung up in bed.

She expected to see Victoria standing over her bed blowing into that stupid whistle. But she wasn't. The sun was low in the sky as it sun shone through the window. It ran across the room and up Gabbie's body making the key hanging around her neck glisten. She picked it up. "I can't believe it! The key came back with me!"

Gabbie flew down the stairs, two at a time. She had to show the key to her sister. She gripped the corner of the wall and used her momentum to propel herself into the kitchen. The table was crowded. Victoria was finishing her supper. Nana was sitting at the table drinking a cup of tea. Two feathers stood behind Nana. I took the empty chair opposite Gabbie's seat, and Madeline hovered over her sister.

"Oh good you're up," Nana said. I fixed you a plate." There was a plate covered with aluminum foil waiting for her on the kitchen counter.

But Gabbie could care less about eating. "Wait 'til you see this!" she said excitedly. She took the key and held it out so her sister could see it. "It's the key to the universe. Mama gave it to me."

Instantly, Nana turned white and choked on her tea.

Chapter Twenty - Three
A Golden Key

"Are you okay?" Gabbie asked, rushing to Nana's side.

The tea had risen up through her throat and out of her nose. "Yes, yes, I'm all right," Nana said with a wave of her hand.

Victoria's eyes peered at the key. "Where did you find that?" she said, sounding annoyed.

Nana and Victoria had searched the whole house looking for the key right after Katherine died. They tore apart every drawer and searched through every box. They pulled up the carpet and moved all the furniture. All they found were sad memories of a mother and daughter, taken to heaven too soon.

Gabbie sighed. "I told you, Mama gave it to me." She twirled the key between her fingers.

"I heard that part," Victoria snapped. "But when?"

Gabbie slapped her leg. "Just now, when I was visiting her in heaven."

Once she was able to speak, Nana told Gabbie that when Katherine was her age, Papa Jim had given her a key exactly like the one hanging around her neck. "Your mom always referred to it as the key to the universe."

"This *is* that key. She took it with her but now she wants me to have. She said it would help to remind me to call on my bubble. It stops the meanies from stealing my energy," Gabbie said swinging the key back and forth. Every time the key crossed the path of sunlight streaming through the kitchen window, the room filled with light. Tiny white lights. Just like the angels made.

"Why would someone want to steal your energy?" Victoria mumbled. She still didn't buy anything Gabbie was selling.

"It's what feeds negativity," Gabbie explained. "I don't think they know that's what they're doing, but they are. So, if I protect myself from people like Melissa, she won't get what she wants. And if she doesn't get what she wants, she'll get tired of bullying me and move on." Gabbie rolled in her lips just as her secret rolled out.

Nana laced her fingers and placed her hands on the table. "Speaking of which," she began. "When you were visiting your mom in heaven, I was chatting with Mr. Ward. He told me what you've been going through and I want to say how sorry I am. I should have known. The tea leaves pointed me in that direction but I doubted my interpretation. If I listened to my intuition we could've come up with a solution. I know how scary bullying can be."

Gabbie felt the same way. If only she had listened to me, she could have spared herself tons of worry. She hadn't realize that keeping this secret had made her so anxious. Finally, the ball in her belly relaxed.

"I do want to know why didn't come to me," Nana said. She patted gabbie's hand. "I'm always here for you."

Gabbie looked down at her lap. She couldn't bare to see her Nana's face when she told her the truth. "I didn't want to be the death of you."

And so a pack was made. Gabbie and Nana twisted their pinky fingers together. "From this moment, I, Gabriella Flowers,...'

"And I, Alice Curtis..., swear to listen to our guides."

Chapter Twenty - Four
A Father's Gift

The following morning, Gabbie kissed her Nana and bravely barreled out the front door. It was a beautiful day. It was the first day since winning the mural contest that Gabbie didn't have a bellyache. The air was filled with the smell of bakery goods and the sun peeked through the cracks between the buildings. Gabbie thought it looked like God's hand stretching down from heaven; each light-filled finger touching his land.

"Good morning, you nasty old cat," Gabbie said as Mr. Fiddlydinks laid in corner of the porch. He rose, but he didn't run away.

That nasty old cat saved your hide yesterday, I said.

"How?" she asked, bewildered.

I told her how Mr. Fiddlydinks had jumped in Melissa's path. How he slowed Melissa down until she had made it home safely.

Gabbie smiled. "You are a nice cat after all." Mr. Fiddlydinks weaved in and out of her legs and for the very first time he let Gabbie pet him.

Ms. Turner stood ready as a crowd of children gathered at the curb, all eager to cross the street. Melissa stood on the other side of the street, waiting. Her foot was tapping wildly. Yet, she didn't know that Gabbie was armed and ready.

Prepare your bubble, I advised. Gabbie raised her arms and encircled herself all while asking God and the angels to protect her. The dragonflies showed up, right on cue. Twinkles of light rained down from the sky, encapsulating her in an invisible bubble.

Now, send her love, I said. Gabbie's eyes narrowed and she bit her bottom lip. It was Melissa whom Gabbie had blamed for taking away her greatest accomplishment, but it was Gabbie herself who replaced it with fear—fear that she, the winner, had graciously received—as well as the prize. So, to send Melissa love was to reclaim a part of herself, a part she didn't know she had given away.

It took a few seconds, but eventually Gabbie gave in. "I ... send you *love,* Melissa Graves." It was a little grumbled, but it was a start.

I swung my arm around her shoulder. Sending love isn't hard to say, in a literal sense, but it can be difficult because of the meaning and power it possesses. To send someone love means to relinquish fear, to honor that person as you honor yourself, because after all, love is the ultimate key. With love, everything is possible. Even dealing with the bully in the classroom.

I'm proud of you, I told her.

Gabbie huffed. *Whatever.*

Even though she didn't want to admit it, her chest warmed and there was a buzzing of happiness in her heart.

We walked across the street. As Melissa approached, Gabbie didn't know what to expect. She wasn't floating in the air like she had in heaven. But I reassured her she was protected just the same.

It didn't take more than two seconds to prove that I was right. Though Melissa was glaring at her, a peaceful feeling washed over Gabbie. Gone were the belly bombs and the tummy twists. The angels did it. They stopped Melissa's negative energy from touching her. A giant smile crossed Gabbie's face. "Thank you, angels," she said. *Thank you.*

Melissa took a step back as we passed her by. Her mouth hung open, disbelieving Gabbie's nerve. "You're such a freak," she hollered as we entered the classroom.

Gabbie smiled. "That's who I am in my heart!"

For the first time since winning the mural contest, Gabbie wouldn't have to contend with Melissa kicking her chair or bouncing rubber bands off the back of her head. She sat peacefully at her desk, unafraid.

"Hey, Gabbie!" Camille shouted. Camille raced toward her, her backpack hanging heavy from her shoulder. "Did you hear Melissa got transferred to Mr. Butler's class?" she whispered excitedly.

"I know, thanks to you," Gabbie said.

Camille shook her head. "It wasn't me," she said. "I'm afraid of Melissa too. It must have been Mrs. Lavish. This was the third time I had a nose bleed this year. And not because you pushed me." She placed her finger on her chin. "Funny though, how it started to bleed right then."

Gabbie grinned. "Angels work in funny ways."

Speaking of angels, I said.

Gabbie snapped her fingers. "Oh, that's right." She used her forefinger to inch Camille closer. "I have to tell you something really important." Camille bent down, anticipating something juicy. She listened intently as Gabbie told her about the pennies Katherine had arranged, and how she had prayed for help. She told her the dragonflies are actually her angels and how she now had a magic bubble. "It protects me against the meanies," she explained.

"Do you think I could have a bubble?" Camille asked wide-eyed. She pushed her glasses up off the edge of her nose.

Gabbie looked at me. I nodded my head. *Anyone can have a bubble. All they have to do is ask.*

The day was super great. Gabbie had no problem paying attention to her studies now that Melissa was gone. Instead of the morning lesson dragging on and on, the time flew by. Before she knew it, she was cleaning up her desk for lunch.

When the bell rang, the students filed out of the classroom. Lunch would be the perfect time to try out their bubbles. Melissa might not be lurking in the classroom, but they couldn't transfer her to another lunch period. All fifth grade classes ate together.

Gabbie spotted Melissa waiting at the front of the food line.

"Prepare your bubble," Gabbie said.

Both girls swung their arms through the air and prayed.

"Now, you have to send her love."

"What?" Camille said. Her eyes were round and unblinking.

"I know it's hard," Gabbie said. "But when I did it, I got a buzzing sensation right here." She pointed at her heart.

Camille pushed her glasses up. "I don't know," she said. Gabbie threw her arm around Camille's shoulder just as I did for her. "I know it's hard, but trust me—it gets easier every time you do it."

Camille sat down in the hallway, right next to Gabbie. "I can't believe those bubbles work," Camille said as Gabbie took her sandwich out of a brown paper bag.

She didn't want to have to turn the rope for Melissa anymore, so she had asked Gabbie if she could help her with the mural. "You know, like squeeze the paint out and wash your brushes and stuff." Gabbie thought it was a great idea. She liked the thought of having an assistant.

"I know, right? It's like we're super heroes, deflecting spears of fear." Gabbie chopped her hands through the air, pretending to deflect negative energy. It was good to see her happy again.

Never again did she have to fear Melissa. Or the food stuck between her teeth. When they walked past her in the lunch line, nothing happened. Oh, don't get me wrong. Melissa still called Gabbie a freak and Camille a snitch, but neither girl had cared.

Chapter Twenty - Five
A Surprising Revelation

*T*he walk home from school was magical. The dragonflies danced overhead. Gabbie and Camille laughed as they twirled through the stardust floating down from the sky. By the time she reached the brownstone, Gabbie was dizzy with laughter.

"See you tomorrow," she said to Camille.

Camille waved. "Thank you for the bubble."

Mr. Fiddlydinks sat on the stoop. He opened one eye as Gabbie raced up the steps. He didn't run away.

Maybe he'll let you pet him, I said.

Gabbie held out her hand. Mr. Fiddlydinks stretched his neck out and rubbed against her fingers. Her eyes grew wide with delight as the cat's throat started to vibrate.

Things sure are different, she told me as she stroked Mr. Fiddlydinks. *Just a few days ago he wouldn't come near me, and now he's purring like mad. I guess I have Melissa to thank.*

A smile crept across my face. Her hand stopped mid-stroke. She tilted her head to the side trying to understand what she had just said. *Could it be true*, she wondered? *Did she owe all of her miracles to the bully in the classroom?* After all, Melissa was the one who had teased her so relentlessly that she had to ask for help, and by doing so she received the bubble of protection. Reaching inside her uniform top, Gabbie pulled out the golden key. She rubbed the key back and forth between her forefinger and thumb, contemplating what she had just uncovered. If it weren't for Melissa, she wouldn't have... the key.

The next day, when Gabbie reached the crossing guard, Melissa stood on the curb, waiting. She snarled when she saw Gabbie walking toward her. Gabbie took a deep breath and rubbed the key for luck. With her bubble in place, she walked up to the meanest girl in school.

"What do you want? Crybaby!" Melissa growled. She loomed over Gabbie, scrambled egg clinging to her wired teeth.

Gabbie rubbed the key again. *Please angels, help me*, she prayed. To her surprise the words began to flow right out of her mouth. "I just wanted to thank you," she said to Melissa. "If it weren't for this experience, I wouldn't have learned about the power of love." She quickly turned to walk away. She was brave, but she was unwilling to hang around Melissa any longer than absolutely necessary.

"*Love?* What's love got to do with it? You're an *idiot!*" Melissa shouted.

That would be the last thing Melissa would say to Gabbie. From that moment on, Melissa Graves, the meanest girl in school, ignored Gabbie completely, as if she didn't exist. Gabbie didn't care. Every time she saw Melissa she closed her eyes and sent her love.

A week later, Principal Ward unveiled the mural. Everyone was there to see it. Gabbie was proud and extremely thankful. It *was* beautiful, if she did say so herself. The dragonflies in the mural glowed as the stardust twinkled. The letters in bright shiny gold read: Be True to Yourself in your Heart.

Camille stood next to Gabbie. She was as proud as Gabbie was. And just as thankful. Gabbie had taken an old key she found on Papa Jim's workbench down in the basement, and hung it on a chain. "This is for you," she had told Camille. "So you always remember the angels have your back." Now both girls have a heavenly reminder.

"It's wonderful, just wonderful!" Nana said, clapping excitedly.

Victoria agreed. "Not bad for a freak." She winked at her sister. Michael even made the trip. He wrapped his arm around Gabbie and pulled her close to his side. "You get your artistic ability from your mother," he said, beaming with pride.

I smiled. Katherine did too.

It was more than just a pretty picture; it was something to live by. Something Gabbie would never forget. And now as the students of Saint Bernadette's started each school day, she hoped that they would also be true to themselves— to have the courage to be who they were in their hearts.

Even though it might take some time for Gabbie to understand why things happened the way they did, I knew there was always something wonderful waiting in the wings.

Gabbie took a deep satisfying breath. She rubbed the key between her fingers. The metal was cool and reassuring. "Now, I'm ready to handle anything that comes my way," she said courageously.

And with that, a penny rolled across the floor and bumped into her shoe.

Acknowledgments

First, I want to thank God, and my angels - without their guidance this book was just a bunch of crumpled pieces of paper tossed at my garbage can.

I want to thank my husband, Rick, who never stopped believing in me. Thanks to my parents for filling my toolbox, for which I am forever grateful.

I want to thank Maryellen Jones and Carla Viotto, who read everything I wrote. Thank you to my critique partner, Joan Sloane, who wandered into my life exactly when I needed her. Thanks to Hope Bookman and Siri German, who helped shape Gabbie in her infancy. Thanks to Deborah Prievo, the most amazing intuitive I know. Without her guidance, I'd still be lost in outer space. I thank Jess Craine for bringing Gabbie to life. Her cover art inspired me. Thank you to all my clients, who listened to my stories for years and gave me ideas and encouragement. We all know the path to publication has been a long one.

Thank you to authors like Sylvia Browne, Doreen Virtue, Carolyn Myss, and Brian Weiss (to name a few), who not only inspired my stories, but also who continue to inspire me in life. To all, I send you my never-ending gratitude, and above all else, I send you love.

CPSIA information can be obtained at www.ICGtesting.com
Printed in the USA
LVOW11*0734261114

415443LV00002B/16/P